VICTOR OSBORNE

MOONDREAM

Lothrop, Lee & Shepard Books
New York

First U. S. Edition published in 1989
1 2 3 4 5 6 7 8 9 10

Library of Congress Cataloging in Publication Data
Osborne, Victor. Moondream.
Summary: When his cousin Katy is kidnapped at night by a Grabbly, Rupert enlists the aid of flying pirates and a kindly badger to rescue her from
the Wizard of Castle Dread. [1. Fantasy] I. Title. PZ7.08134Mo 1989 [Fic]
88-13654   ISBN 0-688-08778-7

In Memory of Ben

Contents

MOONDREAM

The Grabbly

"It's my turn to use the good racket," said Rupert, holding his hand out to Katy.

"No, it's not. I've just won, so it can't be."

"But you're always winning with that one. It's not fair," shouted Rupert. He was red-faced and hot from playing tennis in the garden, and his feelings of injustice were making him even hotter.

"It's very fair." Katy laughed. "If the winner can't keep the best racket there'd be no point in winning." She twirled the racket in Rupert's face. It had a string missing, but it was a proper one, unlike Rupert's, which was heavy plastic and harder to hit with.

Rupert threw his racket on the ground and

snatched at Katy's. She quickly put it behind her back.

"You're just a bad loser. Bad loser. Bad loser," she taunted him, dancing about to stop Rupert from getting behind her.

"Give it to me," he panted.

"You've got to win it fair and square, otherwise you can't have it."

"Oh, yes I can," cried Rupert, and he leaped forward with outstretched hands to snatch the racket over Katy's head, but he was out of breath and couldn't leap high enough. His hands pushed into Katy's shoulders and she went over backward into the goldfish pond, letting go of the racket as she fell. The pond was only a few inches deep, but it was enough to soak her right through.

Rupert was in disgrace. He was sent to bed without supper, which was sure to give him bad dreams in the night. He didn't care. He'd got the tennis racket from Katy, and that was what was important. Wasn't it?

As he sat on his bed cradling the racket, he began to wonder whether it was so important after all. He still felt that Katy should have given him a turn. But it was only a game. He shouldn't have pushed her into the water. If she was very upset and decided she didn't like him anymore, who would he play with tomorrow?

The cottage he lived in stood by itself on a hillside, almost surrounded by a cornfield that swept in a golden carpet down into the valley where the woods began, Willowherb Woods— greenly dark and mysterious, a forbidden place to play. There was nobody else living nearby, which was why Rupert always looked forward to Katy's visits in the school holidays.

She was a sort of cousin, a little bit younger than he, and they enjoyed the same things, like looking for birds' nests and magic circles of mushrooms in hidden places on the hillside.

Rupert had shown her where a grass snake slept in the afternoon sun, and Katy didn't like it and burst into tears. Rupert laughed and called her a scaredy cat, but when he saw that she really *was* scared he made her a daisy chain to show that he was sorry. Katy took the red velvet ribbon out of her hair and wore the chain as a garland. Rupert said she looked like a princess, and they were friends once more.

Would they be again? Rupert got into bed

feeling miserable. His tummy was hollow and achy. It was a warm evening and the windows and curtains were open. A harvest moon, as big as a balloon, edged up over the windowsill. Far away a dog barked at it. Rupert turned over and tried not to think about food.

He *did* have a bad dream, and it was a stinker. He was in a strange house and shapeless monsters were creeping up on him. In the dream he turned his head from side to side to try to see them, but they were always quicker, dodging out of sight, ready to come after him again when he looked away. He ran from room to room. They ran too, all the time coming closer and closer. They wanted to grab him. They were Grabblies.

He cried out in his dream, "Help, help! Please, somebody help me. Oh, won't someone help me? Please, please!"

It was too late, he was going to be grabbed.

No, he wasn't. Someone had heard his cry for help.

Rupert woke up as the door of his bedroom was thrown open. He opened his eyes and saw Katy, wearing a nightgown and with the red ribbon in her hair, run into the room. She flung herself at the Grabbly. It had been standing by the bed, its webbed arms raised up, casting a deep shadow over him as he slept. It staggered back toward the bottom of the bed and the window as Katy attacked it, slapping and kicking in a wild fury.

Rupert sat up. He was still dopey with sleep. He heard Katy shout, "Get away, you horrible thing!" and pant with the effort of driving it back. He saw her snatch at one of her slippers to use as a weapon—but while she was distracted the Grabbly lunged forward and grabbed her.

It carried her to the window and for a moment it was outlined in bright moonlight. It was a terrible sight, like a moving sack of potatoes. It even had a knobbly brown potato skin. Wisps of swamp steam rose from cracks in the skin. It had no head, yet a face appeared. The features rippled over the uneven surface until two eyes, a nose, and a wide gash of a mouth came together to scowl at Rupert. He shrank back. Two arms held Katy, two more grasped the window frame. The mouth snarled in triumph as the Grabbly launched itself out the window. In that instant, as if in a photograph, Rupert saw Katy

5

struggling in the Grabbly's grip, her face defiant, refusing to show fear.

The grogginess left Rupert and he leaped out of bed. Too late; and this time it really *was* too late.

He reached the window and looked into the garden. There was no sign of them. He looked everywhere. They weren't there.

He looked up. Far away there was a small cloud. It was the only one in the sky and it was traveling very fast. Sticking out behind it were two legs, kicking. Only one of the feet had a slipper on.

The cloud dwindled to a dot as it went to the west over Willowherb Woods. Then it veered to the north and disappeared.

Rupert stared after it. Slowly he became aware of the silence of the house, broken by a ticking clock downstairs. Amazingly, Katy had been spirited away without anyone else in the house knowing about it.

The harvest moon cast its silvery light over the peaceful countryside. The smell of honeysuckle came up from the garden, mixed with fainter, earthier smells from the cornfield. It was so peaceful and normal that Rupert began to wonder if he had dreamed it all.

He thought, Katy's probably asleep in her bed. If she is, I'll know it was only a nightmare. He went to the open door and crossed the landing. Katy's door was also open. The covers of the bed were thrown aside. It was empty.

Rupert ran back. By the bottom of his bed lay a slipper. He stared at it, suddenly feeling cold and lost in his own snug room. It hadn't been a dream. He walked unsteadily across the floor and picked the slipper up. It was still warm from Katy's foot. It was small and soft. He turned it over. A flower, which he recognized as a poppy, was embroidered over the toes.

He looked up at the sky. Katy had fought to save him. Now, somehow, he had to save her.

"I'll get you back, Katy. I promise," he said, speaking aloud for the reassurance of hearing his voice. He had no idea what to do.

Rupert was about to close the window when a shadow passed across the moon. Was the monster bringing her back? Or was it returning for him? Quickly he looked around for something to defend himself with. The only thing he could find in a hurry was the tennis racket. It would have to do.

"Come on, Grabbly," he said. "I'm ready

for you." He sounded a lot braver than he felt, what with butterflies fluttering in his tummy.

But the sight that met his eyes was no monster. Floating across the face of the moon came a ship in full sail. Rupert stared open-mouthed with astonishment. What could it be this time?

The Flying Pirates

The ship heaved and plunged as she traveled through the air. Up and down. Up and down. She rolled, too, from side to side, while the billowing sails shook and rippled. A wake of bubbles trailed out mistily from the stern.

She was on a course that would take her past the garden, over the meadow, and across the woods.

"Ahoy, there." The call was faint. Rupert saw a shape at the ship's side. It was too far away to make out clearly, but he thought he saw an arm waving.

"Ahoy, there." The call was repeated.

Rupert waved the racket in reply. A moment later the ship heeled around as she changed course toward him. The sails were reefed, and the vessel slowed down and became steadier. She sank slowly through the air as she approached the house. Down and down, growing bigger and bigger. By the time she crossed the garden fence, the ship was level with the roof.

The ship's prow slipped past the window. Rupert caught a quick glimpse of the figurehead. It was a pig. A green pig dressed in a flowered waistcoat and waving its trotters in the air.

"Let go the anchor!" It was the same voice, deeper and gruffer at close quarters. There was a rattle of chain, followed by the sound of breaking glass from the greenhouse below. With a creaking of timbers the ship stopped and hove to in midair, almost close enough for Rupert to lean out and touch.

He did. At least, he prodded at it carefully with the tennis racket to see if it was real. Tap, tap. It was.

"Aha, me hearty. You'd need to give *The Dainty Duck* a pretty whack to make her bounce."

Startled, Rupert looked up. Standing at the ship's railing was a large grizzled dog wearing a long blue jacket with gold stripes down the front. A three-cornered hat was tipped back on his head. He looked friendly enough, but there was something lopsided about him. His ears. Rupert noticed that the left one flopped down while the right one stood up and was missing the tip. It gave him a weatherbeaten, battle-scarred look.

"Not that tennis is my game," the dog went on. "Bowls. A steady hand, a keen eye, and a fine sense of judgment is what's needed for bowls. There's a game for a sailor. When he's on shore, of course. Which, praise St. Bernard, I'm not often."

Rupert couldn't think of anything to say to this, so he just nodded.

"Yes. Well, there I go, off on a tack. I am Captain Bones. At your service." He took his hat off with a flourish, then replaced it even farther back on his head.

"I'm Rupert," said Rupert. "You are real, aren't you?"

"Why, of course I be real. I think." The dog looked worried. "Here, I'll pinch myself to make sure." Captain Bones put a paw to his right ear and pinched. "Ouch. There, I be real all right." He rubbed his ear tenderly.

"Only, a monster got into my bedroom. I didn't know if I was dreaming. Then it carried off Katy. She's my cousin. When I saw you coming, I thought—"

"A monster?" Captain Bones said sharply. He stopped rubbing his ear. "What sort of a monster would that be?"

Members of the crew who had gathered around the Captain pressed forward expectantly. The audience made Rupert unsure of himself.

"Come on, lad. What was it?" the Captain said kindly but firmly.

Thinking about it set off feelings of panic again. "I don't know what it was," Rupert burst out. "It was horrible, shapeless. I don't know how it got into my room, but it grabbed Katy and flew out the window with her. It flew off very quickly, high up in the sky. I don't know where she is, and I . . . I . . . I don't know what to do." He breathed in big gulps as he tried to swallow the panic before it reached his throat.

"A Grabbly," said the Captain, slapping the handrail. "I knew we were getting close." He saw how upset Rupert was. "Easy, lad, you've had a nasty shock. Those Grabblies be so awful they'd make a stone statue shiver. You go and lie down, but first would you show me which way it went?"

Rupert leaned out the window and pointed toward the north. "Over there."

"We'll catch it, the devil," Captain Bones said grimly. "And when we do . . ." The threat seemed all the more terrible for being left unspoken. He turned and shouted, "All hands on deck! Prepare to weigh anchor."

Rupert knew this was his big chance to rescue Katy, and nothing was going to stop him.

"Captain! Captain," he called. Captain Bones swung around. "Let me go with you."

The sea-dog pulled at the fur under his chin.

"It'll be dangerous work," he said doubtfully. "Besides, you'll be missed." He nodded toward the house.

"I must find Katy. The Grabbly got her because she was trying to help me. Now it's my turn to help her. If you won't take me, I'll still have to look for her. So please let me go with you. I promise I won't get in the way."

Captain Bones looked down at Rupert from under gray-flecked, wind-tangled eyebrows.

"All right," he said at last. A gangplank

13

was pushed across to the windowsill. Rupert put Katy's slipper carefully inside his pajama top and took a firm grip on the tennis racket. He climbed onto the plank, walked quickly along it, and was helped onto the deck. The gangplank was pulled in behind him.

Sailors were hurrying about getting the ship ready. Rupert had never been on a sailing ship before. It looked enormously exciting.

Captain Bones laid a paw on his shoulder. "Welcome aboard *The Dainty Duck,* shipmate. She's as fine a vessel as ever sailed the seven winds."

"Don't you mean the seven seas?" said Rupert.

The dog tapped his muzzle with a claw. "I knows what I mean, and I mean what I say." Then, when he saw that Rupert was completely mystified, he added, "We be flying pirates," as if this explained everything.

"Did you say flying pirates? But how do you fly?"

Captain Bones smiled, and his floppy ear went up and down.

"Dreams. Children's dreams. The air is full of them, going this way and that. We hoist our sails and a dream comes along and off we go. It's just like the wind, only they buoy us up as well as drive us along."

"I never knew that dreams flew about," said Rupert. "I thought you went to sleep and just had them."

"Why, bless you, boy, no," said the Captain. "Dreams be busy things. They go from one sleeping child to another, changing a bit each time so no dream ever repeats itself. Some of them whiz along full of excitement, others float slow and lazy."

"Can you see them and pick which one you want, slow or fast? I sometimes try to pick a dream before I go to sleep. I don't usually get it, though."

"No more do we. A dream only lets you see it when you're asleep. We never know what we've got till it's in the sails. Come with me and we'll see what we get this time."

The Captain led the way to the stern, where he took hold of the wheel and barked to the waiting crew, "Hoist the mainsail!"

Sailors leaped about pulling on ropes. In a moment the great white mainsail had unfolded. It hung limply at first. Then it began to fill out from the center, the canvas sighing as it stretched, the timbers creaking as they took the strain. Slowly *The Dainty Duck* got under way. Rupert saw his bedroom window edge back beyond the rail. The rest of the house followed more quickly.

Captain Bones spun the wheel to the left. The ship's bow turned in that direction, but to Rupert it seemed as if the ship remained still while the house, the garden fences, the cornfield, and the distant woods turned around it. The Captain pulled on the wheel and *The Dainty Duck* started to rise as she moved forward.

The Captain ordered more sails to be set. Rupert asked him what sort of dream they had caught. The Captain sniffed the air once or twice. "A calm, peaceful dream—maybe one that has followed on from a bedtime story."

"That thing in my bedroom, the Grabbly," began Rupert. "I thought I was dreaming when I saw it. You know, having a nightmare." He shivered.

"I'm not surprised," said the Captain. "I've seen a fair few of them things and each one looks worse than the last. Not that I've ever been able to get as close as I'd like, which is close enough to give them a taste of shot." And he growled deep in his chest.

"What are they?" asked Rupert. "And what are they doing?"

The dog scratched behind his right ear. "I don't rightly know the answer to your first question. It's a puzzler—eh, Mr. Mate?"

The mate, a terrier with a patch over one eye, agreed. "It's a mystery we'll only solve when we catch one of them."

"Which we will, by thunder."

"Is that why you're chasing them, to find out what they are? Or because they grab people? Have they grabbed some of your crew?" Rupert asked.

"Hold on, lad. Drop your anchor. All these questions. You're making me as dizzy as a moth in a lighthouse." Captain Bones swept the rigging with a practiced eye, as if to get his balance back. Then he looked at Rupert. "We don't know where the Grabblies come from or where they go to. They only started appearing a little while ago, but they do a terrible mischief to the dreams. They're like miniature typhoons, raising contrary winds and whirlpools in the air.

"We don't know when or where they're going to crop up. Every time they do, they have us storm-driven all over the sky. We haven't been able to do a decent bit of piracy for weeks. We have to find them and make them stop it, by friendly persuasion, *or . . .*" Here the Captain looked meaningfully toward the gun deck. "Because if it goes on much longer we'll be put out of business as flying pirates. Then it will be the end for us."

Rupert could see that things looked desperate for *The Dainty Duck* and her crew.

Macaroni and Cheese

There was a stir down by the bow. The green pig Rupert had glimpsed earlier was pulling himself unsteadily over the ship's side. He reached the ship's rail and paused to draw breath.

Everyone stopped doing whatever they were doing to watch.

"That's the third mate," said the Captain, coming out of his gloomy reverie.

"Scoundrels," squealed the pig weakly. "Rogues. You have been beastly to me and I resign from the crew now and straightaway. So there."

He stamped a trotter. It slipped on the polished wood. He lost his balance and fell heavily to the deck.

19

Rupert hurried over. The pig was lying in a heap, eyes closed, and breathing heavily. His snout twitched once or twice and he muttered, "For shame, for shame. A pig must have his dignity."

Rupert decided that he wasn't hurt, just winded from the fall. He had never seen a green pig before. Such a shiny, rich green, like the skin of an apple. Green and fat. As fat as a barrel.

The waistcoat he was wearing, which was as tight as a second skin, was the most colorful piece of clothing Rupert had ever seen. Pink, blue, white, and yellow flowers flowed and whirled over it. They merged into one another at some points and erupted away from one another elsewhere. A border of black and red thread tried to keep the flowers in check. Down the back of the waistcoat ran a broad zigzag of salmon pink between butter-colored stripes.

The crew gathered around. When the pig had recovered his breath, he stood up shakily.

In the tone of a person who has suffered great injury to his pride, he said, "Why do you shame me, Captain? I, the descendant of a great and noble line of Roman pigs, tied up like a common swine. Such indignity."

Two tears squeezed out of the corners of his eyes and ran down his green cheeks. A sympathetic murmur came from the crew. Captain Bones shuffled his boots in embarrassment.

Rupert whispered to one of the crew, "What happened?"

"We take turns being the figurehead since the real figurehead was shot off in a battle. We were going to draw straws to see who should do it this time, and Porko ate them. They were cheese straws. So the Captain made him be the figurehead. He doesn't normally take turns because of his health."

The pig went on in a more fretful voice, "You know I can't stand heights. I feel quite dizzy from that climb up the anchor chain. Dizzy and faint. A morsel to eat would restore me and take away the taste of that horrible rope I had to nibble through." A pink tongue licked along green lips.

"There's nothing left in the galley," said the cook, "excepting some stale bread and dried prunes."

The pig rolled his eyes and snorted. "Ugh."

Rupert felt quite sorry for him. He knew what it was like to go hungry. "We were having macaroni and cheese for supper, only I didn't have any, so there must be some left if we can go back for it."

Rupert had touched a subject dear to the pig's heart.

"Macaroni and cheese!" the pig exclaimed with ecstasy. "Macaroni and cheese. My favorite. The food of Roman emperors."

His snout began to twitch with excitement. His eyes opened wide and he noticed Rupert for the first time.

"Who are you?" he said.

"I'm Rupert."

"You have, sir, the honor of addressing Il Porko, a noble Roman pig. A beast that is most partial to macaroni and cheese."

The repeated mention of macaroni and cheese was too much for Porko's tummy. It rumbled like distant thunder. Then it gurgled like bathwater running out. Rumble, rumble, gurgle.

Porko forgot about his dignity. "Rupert, my friend, my dear, dear friend. You must fetch it. A morsel, a plateful, a bowlful."

"It's at the house," said Rupert. "And, look, it's a long way away now." They looked. *The Dainty Duck* had picked up speed and height. She was well over the cornfield, and the house was quite small in the distance behind them.

Porko did a little hop on the deck. He waved his forelegs in agitation. "Oh, my! Captain, we must go back, please. It will only take a minute. If we don't I'll fade away with hunger."

Captain Bones stood there undecided. Then the decision was made for him. *The Dainty Duck* shivered from stem to stern as if a big wave had crashed into her. At the same time the lookout in the crow's nest shouted, "Grabbly, ho. Off the starboard bow."

They ran to the side. In the distance they saw a small black cloud. It was higher than they were and moving much faster. As it traveled through the air it constantly changed shape.

Captain Bones let out an oath. "Bluebeard's whiskers! There'll be no turning back now." He shouted to the crew, "Action stations! Run out the guns!

"Come on," he said grimly to Rupert, leading the way to the stern. "We'll see how that Grabbly likes the whiff of shot."

The ship turned in pursuit of the distant

Grabbly that was hurrying to terrify some poor sleeping child. More sails were hoisted until *The Dainty Duck* was fairly shooting through the sky. Gun ports were opened and cannons were trundled out, loaded, and primed for firing.

Captain Bones was striding backward and forward in great excitement, shouting encouragement to the crew and the ship and threats at the Grabbly. In between he put his brass-bound telescope to his eye to measure the distance between them.

The Dainty Duck strained her timbers and stretched her canvas in the effort to catch up. But the dream in her sails simply wasn't pushing hard enough, and it was soon plain to see, even without a brass telescope, that they were dropping behind. The black cloud got smaller and smaller until it vanished from sight.

With an angry gesture, Captain Bones swung his telescope down. The heavy ring around the lens caught him on the shin with a loud crack.

"Sea-cats!" he howled, clutching his injured leg and hopping around on the other. "Sea-rats, sea-snakes!"

Rupert thought this would be a good time to be somewhere else. He made his way forward

24

to the mainmast and was wondering what to do when he heard a voice singing sadly from behind the jolly boat.

There was Porko, sitting on a coil of rope, holding a shriveled prune in one hand, and chewing on a stale crust of bread. He stopped chewing and started to sing again in a wobbly voice,

> "Porko is an aeronaut,
> A most amazing flying sort
> Of death-defying pig.
> What acrobatic artistry
> To scorn the pull of gravity,
> And dance an airborne jig."

Here he shuffled his back legs in a poor imitation of an Irish jig. His heart wasn't in it.

"Hello, Porko," said Rupert.

"Hello, dear boy," said the pig, attempting unsuccessfully to smile. "I was trying to cheer myself up. Life does seem a bit hard on a pig at times." He sighed again.

Rupert sat down beside him. "I'm awfully sorry about the macaroni and cheese."

"Ah, the macaroni and cheese," Porko said gloomily.

"We *could* have gone back. It wouldn't have made any difference."

"Don't, don't. I can't bear to think about it."

There was a heavy silence.

"It's just that I'm feeling hungry too," said Rupert. "I was sent to bed without any supper."

"My dear boy. How terrible. Here I've been, wrapped up in my own tummy, so to speak, while you've been suffering in silence. Share this with me. Half a crust is better than no crust at all, eh? At least, that's what they say." He gave Rupert a piece of bread. "What are you doing on this ship? I don't remember you coming aboard."

Rupert told him about the Grabbly and how Katy had fought it before being carried off. He brought her slipper out from his pajama top to show Porko.

"Bellissimo. Such bravery," murmured the pig, deeply impressed by the story.

Rupert explained that he had vowed to find Katy and bring her back, and told how he had hailed *The Dainty Duck* and persuaded Captain Bones to take him along. "That happened while you were still tied up as the figurehead."

26

Porko shuddered. "I've a good mind to report the Captain to the ASPCA for that."

"The ASPCA . . .?"

"The American Society for Pigs to be Cherished Always. You must have heard of it."

"Oh, yes." Rupert knew about the ASPCA but hadn't been sure what the initials stood for.

Suddenly they were pitched head over heels as *The Dainty Duck* lurched to a stop amid the sound of splintering wood. Porko skidded on his back up to the ship's side, bounced off, and got jammed under the jolly boat. Rupert was flung against him. By the time he staggered to his feet everything was in chaos. Sails and ropes hung down. Barrels and boxes had been smashed, and several of the cannons had tipped over.

About a dozen of the crew were fetched up around the mainmast in a jumble of striped jerseys, spotted scarves, and checked trousers. They looked like a pile of washing.

What happened? wondered Rupert in alarm.

Into the Woods

The heap of sailors around the mast stirred. Then the heap shivered. One or two of the sailors at the top slid down. The shiver became more violent. The heap shook with internal convulsions and fell apart as Captain Bones heaved himself up from the bottom.

He stood there unsteadily, his three-cornered hat jammed over his eyes.

"Have we been boarded?" he roared, pulling out his cutlass and laying about him with wild swipes. The crew scattered.

"Captain, Captain," cried the mate, "it's not boarders. We've run aground."

"What? A reef, is it? All hands to the boats. Watch out for sharks."

"No, Cap'n. Your hat's over your eyes. If you take it off and come to the side you'll see what's happened."

He did so.

Below *The Dainty Duck* were trees, their tops nearly brushing her keel. There were trees as far as the eye could see. Bushy trees, spiky trees, and stately spreading trees. The crown of each one caught the moonlight in its leaves, reflecting a thousand thousand splinters of silver light. Lower down, the silver turned to a dappled gray before disappearing altogether into the deep gloom. But the crowns glittered and sparkled. It could have been a stormy sea in which the waves and spray had been frozen in an instant.

It was an astonishing sight, though it wasn't what the mate had called them over for. He was pointing toward the bow. "The anchor chain. Do you see? It runs out from the ship as stiff as an iron rod. We've anchored ourselves in those woods."

"No wonder we pulled up with such a wallop," said Captain Bones, leaning out from the side to peer into the darkness below. "What I want to know is, how did it happen? We were all shipshape and Bristol fashion back there. The anchor was lashed up as normal. I can't make it out."

With a shock Rupert realized that Katy's slipper was missing. Oh, no, no, he thought. Not that, not his link with Katy. He'd been holding it to show Porko, so he must have dropped it when they stopped. He looked around the deck. No sign of it. In growing panic Rupert felt inside his pajama top. No slipper. There could only be one explanation, and it was dreadful, like losing Katy herself. The slipper must have gone over the side and fallen into the dark woods below.

Porko, meanwhile, was untangling himself from coils of rope, which reminded the Captain of something.

"Porko," he said thoughtfully, "what rope did you chew through when you were in the bows?"

"I don't know, Captain. There was rope everywhere. I just chewed and chewed until it all fell away. It tasted horrible." He squirmed at the memory and pulled a sour lemon face. "Why?"

"Why? Because you must have chewed the

30

rope holding the anchor secure, that's why. Haven't you got any sense?"

"You mean that crash . . . the anchor . . ."

Captain Bones nodded grimly. "Right. Take a pick and a shovel. Climb down that chain and free the anchor."

"Me? Climb down there? But I can't stand heights," wailed the poor pig.

"I don't care. It's your fault we're stuck, so you'll have to unstick us."

Porko looked down into the dark woods, gulped, and turned to the Captain appealingly. "Me?"

"Yes, you. And be quick about it."

"Here," said one of the crew, roughly passing him a spade and a pickax. "Take these."

"I'll come with you," said Rupert quickly, seizing his chance. He had to get that slipper back somehow. He knew that while he had it, he and Katy would find each other. Without it they were both lost.

The anchor chain was made up of large iron links, which provided good foot- and handholds. Rupert went first, carrying the tennis racket awkwardly in his left hand. In a minute he had climbed down among the topmost branches and *The Dainty Duck* was hidden from view.

It wasn't as dark on the floor of Willow-herb Woods as it had seemed from above. The moonlight that was so bright up there was mostly screened out by the trees, but enough filtered through to see by. In places, moonbeams shone through gaps in the leaves, splashing pools of light on the ground.

The anchor had dug itself into a tangle of roots around a massive oak tree that stood alone in a small clearing.

Rupert jumped the last few feet to the ground, then helped Porko down. "That's going to take a lot of digging out," Rupert said.

There wasn't a sound in the woods.

"Maybe there are Things out there," whispered Porko after a while.

"What sort of Things?"

"I don't know. Things."

"You mean like the Grabblies?"

"Worse than that. Things that eat little pigs. You'd never know until they jumped out. Then it would be too late." Porko's voice had been rising as he spoke. He ended on a high-pitched squeak.

Rupert was beginning to feel nervous too.

Things that ate pigs probably had boys for dessert.

"Come on, help me with this anchor," he said. "The sooner we free it, the sooner we can go."

They started to dig. When the hardest part was done, Rupert told Porko he was going to have a look for the slipper.

"Do be careful," said the pig, his nervousness returning. "Keep a lookout for you-know-what."

Rupert said he would. He crossed the clearing in a few steps and set off through the trees, following the track that had been gouged along the ground by the dragging anchor. Branches that had been broken off by the chain lay alongside the track.

Rupert counted his paces, all the time looking to either side. When he reached a hundred he stopped. It couldn't have been this far back. But he'd looked carefully and there had been no sign of the slipper. He turned slowly until he was facing the way he had come. The woods were very still.

Suddenly it came to him. He had been looking in the wrong direction. If the anchor was trailing behind the ship, the ship must have been in front of it when the anchor snagged in the roots and the shock sent the slipper flying over the side. Of course!

Rupert ran back. In the clearing, Porko was standing in the hole they had dug, levering the anchor out from among the roots. He was huffing and puffing with the effort. The chain was moving slightly as if being shaken from above.

Rupert ran past him. "I won't be a minute. Wait for me."

The trees grew more thickly on the other side. He slowed to a walk and began to count his paces . . . eighteen, nineteen, twenty, twenty-one. . . . Less light came through here. It was difficult to see more than a couple of feet on either side before darkness came down like a curtain . . . thirty-three, thirty-four, thirty-five, thirty-six. The trees grew closer and closer together. What was that noise?

Rupert stopped. He could feel his heart beating. The woods had been still and silent until a moment ago. Now a sound was filling them, a distant sighing sound. Like waves breaking on a pebbly beach. Or the breathing of something very big.

"There aren't Things in the woods," he said

aloud. "It'll be the wind. That's what it is." He made himself walk on . . . forty-nine, fifty, fifty-one, fifty-two. . . . The sound was getting louder.

I must find the slipper, thought Rupert. I *must.* It had become a sort of talisman. A symbol of his determination to find Katy and rescue her.

He walked a little farther. The woods were coming alive with rustlings and moanings. It was darker than ever. Suppose Porko was right and there *were* Things living here?

Rupert couldn't walk another step. The trees were moving, swaying, reaching, closing in around him. The woods had become a terrifying place. A place to get out of as quickly as possible. He turned to run.

It was then that he saw the slipper. His eye was drawn by the red of the embroidered poppy on the toe. The slipper had fallen into some branches a little above head level.

In a flash Rupert snatched it down and was running as fast as he could. Twigs snatched like fingers at his pajamas. Brambles pulled at his feet. He ran and ran, his ears full of the woods' roaring.

He burst into the clearing at full speed, in

time to see the anchor hoisted up off the ground. Rupert came to a stop by the edge of the freshly dug hole. There was no sign of Porko. Looking up, he caught a last glimpse of the anchor disappearing among the tossing treetops. He was alone in the witchery woods.

Badger

The summer storm that had blown up out of a clear sky lashed through the woods. Rupert threw himself full length among the gnarled old tree roots. He wasn't going to cry. He was going to be brave and resourceful and plan what to do next.

The tears came anyway. Alone in the woods, with his face pressed against the warm-smelling earth, Rupert wept out his fears.

Why had he joined the flying pirates if they were going to abandon him? Why hadn't he gone to Katy's help before the Grabbly had a chance to carry her away? Why, oh why, oh why?

Too much had happened too quickly. He was overwhelmed by it all.

By and by the tears stopped, and he felt better.

He was wondering what had happened to Porko when he heard the pig singing in a muffled voice.

"Porko! Porko, thank goodness," shouted Rupert. He jumped up with delight and looked around the clearing. The pig was nowhere in sight.

"Where are you? I thought you might have gone up to the ship with the anchor."

"I came down with the anchor," said the muffled voice.

"What are you talking about?"

"I was pulling the anchor out the last inch when up it went, knocking me backward off my trotters. I tumbled over and over and over, bumping all the way. I feel quite bruised and not cherished at all."

"Maybe you've fallen down a rabbit hole. Keep talking and I'll try to find you."

It had become darker since the storm began. Rupert moved forward, tapping on the ground in front of him with the tennis racket.

The pig cleared his throat with a few "ahems" and began a new song.

"I've knocked about the world all right,
We flying pirates keep amused,
The world has knocked me back tonight,
I'm bumped and bruised and much abused."

That's closer. A bit over to the right, Rupert reckoned.

"Pigs were never meant to fly,
Mum's advice to me was sound,
But I had to go and try,
Now I'm stuck here underground."

The rabbit hole was almost beneath the oak tree, not far from the one they had dug. Rupert knelt at the edge and felt inside it. There was a wooden ledge, and another. They were steps. He swung his feet down.

Porko stopped his sorrowful singing when he saw Rupert. "I'd started to think I'd fallen into a trap made by those Things and one of them was coming for me. But it was you, and this is only an old rabbit hole. Aren't I silly?" He giggled.

Rupert reached the bottom. It was very dark. He put out a hand and touched the pig.

39

Porko gave a squeal of pretend fright. He was sitting with his back against something. Rupert touched that too. It was wood, rough planks, and there was a handle.

"I don't think it *is* an old rabbit hole," he said slowly. "There are steps, for one thing. I've never heard of rabbits making steps. And another thing. There's a door down here. You're leaning against it." The pig jumped away as if the door had become red hot.

"What's that noise?" Rupert said.

"What noise? I can't hear anything. You're trying to scare me, aren't you?" Porko laughed nervously.

"No. Listen."

From behind the door came a shuffling sound. Faint at first, but growing louder. Chinks of light appeared through the cracks between the planks. The shuffling stopped, to be replaced after a moment by a scraping and scratching.

"Come on," squealed Porko. "I knew this was a Thing trap. Let's get out of here."

"All right. Follow me," and Rupert led a mad scramble up the steps.

Porko was all for running off across the clearing into the trees. Rupert stopped him. His curiosity had returned. He wanted to see what was down there. Then they could run if they had to.

They flopped down among the roots a little way from the opening and waited to see what would appear.

From below the ground came the rasp of heavy iron bolts being pulled back. There was a rusty screech of old hinges, and with a graveyard groan the door underneath the oak tree was opened.

Yellow light spilled out, faint and wavery. It grew stronger, turning the hole into a flickering golden pool. Strange shadows darted about the clearing, giant bats swooping and vanishing only to reappear from unexpected angles. Huge birds with flashing beaks were swept away into darkness a split second before they struck. Snakes writhed out of the earth, twisting and slithering along the ground and into the trees with furious speed as the light turned on them.

Porko was frightened beyond words. He couldn't have squealed if his life depended on it. He was too frightened even to think of covering his eyes to blot out the awful sights. This was worse than Grabblies.

Rupert's curiosity disappeared very quickly. He could feel Porko trembling violently as if he had a chill.

The Thing was climbing up. Each wooden step creaked under its weight. Creak, scratch, creak, scratch. Could that be claws on the wood?

The beams of light rushed together, became a beacon. Steady and bright. The flickering shadows stilled. Birds and bats and snakes turned back into leaves and branches and roots.

Some earth and pebbles slipped into the hole where the anchor had been.

"Vandals," said a voice from behind the light.

Rupert strained to make out the shape of the speaker. It was vague and not very reassuring.

"Vandals," the voice repeated. "Probably those weasel cubs. Digging a hole outside my back door for me to fall into. If I catch those young rascals, I'll give them what for."

The next moment something that looked like a spotted tablecloth fluttered about the light.

"Aashoo! Aaashoo oo!" The sound of an explosive sneeze filled the clearing.

Rupert was so startled he jabbed the pig's snout with the tennis racket.

"Wheee," yelped Porko, jumping all of two inches off the ground.

"Who's there? Come out where I can see you. Digging holes in my backyard. We'll see about that."

The light was held up and directed around the tree. Rupert tried to shrink back among the tangle of roots, but it was no good. He and Porko were picked out and held in a steady beam.

"Well, I'm blowed. It's a boy. What's that with you? A dog? Must say, it's a funny-looking dog."

When there was no reply, the speaker asked in a more kindly tone, "What are you doing here, boy, in the woods at this time of night? It's no place for children. Are you lost? Is that it?"

Rupert was thinking, This definitely does not sound like a Thing that goes around gobbling up pigs and little boys. He felt Porko trembling beside him and was reminded that you couldn't be too sure. He took a fresh grip on the tennis racket.

"I'm Rupert and this is Porko. We are flying pirates. Who are you?" he asked, holding his free hand up against the glare of the light.

"Dear me, I'm forgetting my manners."

Shutters were opened on the lamp.

"Is that better? Can you see now?"

Indeed he could. What Rupert saw was a long pointed head. It began or finished—he wasn't sure which—with a large black nose. The strangest thing about it was the black and white stripes that ran up the face. A pair of dark eyes regarded the boy and the pig with interest.

The creature seemed to have no neck. Where the head finished the body began, a powerful, heavily built body clad in a smart gray furry coat. A huge handkerchief printed with whirls of color hung down from a pocket. The arms were muscular, ending in paws that possessed the largest claws Rupert had ever seen. He had no doubt that they could make short work of a pig or two if the owner had a mind. The left paw held up an oil lamp. The right clutched a walking stick.

"I'm Badger," said the creature.

"How do you do," said Rupert, on his best behavior.

Porko, who was sufficiently reassured to

feel very put out at being mistaken for a dog, said rather rudely, "You're not a Thing, then."

"I beg your pardon?" said Badger.

"What he means," explained Rupert, "is, you don't go around eating pigs and, er, other people, do you?"

The reply was a chuckle, a rich, rumbling, throaty sound. It went up in pitch and became a giggle. Then Badger threw his head back and let the laughter roar out. He shook so much with merriment he clutched his sides to keep them from splitting. The lamp bounced and bumped against his coat, throwing out sparks.

"Eat people, me?" Badger gasped at length, trying to catch his breath. "What a thought," and he started to laugh again.

"I didn't think it was funny," said Porko huffily. He twitched his snout. "Can you smell something?"

Rupert could. Smoke was curling around the lamp.

"Excuse me," he said loudly. "I think you're on fire."

"On fire?" repeated Badger, apparently not taking in the sense of what he was saying.

Then he noticed the smoke that was beginning to billow up around his head. "Good heavens," he said with alarm. "I'm on fire. I'm burning."

Badger dropped the lamp and the stick and started to beat at his coat with his paws.

The agitated animal was almost hidden by smoke and showering sparks. Rupert had seen a red glow at the center of it. He dashed forward, grabbed a corner of the handkerchief, pulled it out of Badger's pocket, and threw it on the ground, where Porko stamped on it until the last spark had gone out.

When the smoke had cleared, Badger shuffled forward.

He bent down, got hold of the handkerchief by two corners, and held it up. It was a sorry sight. The middle had been burned right out, leaving a ragged black-edged hole.

"Ruined," said Badger sadly. "And it was my best handkerchief."

He put it carefully back into his pocket, picked up the lamp and the stick, and turned to go back the way he had come.

Porko and Rupert looked at each other. What should they do now?

The storm was blowing through the treetops as strongly as ever. The first raindrops found their way through the leaves. Large, soft drops that fell with slow plops onto the ground. Rupert felt one on his hand, then his cheek. Another landed on Porko's neck and trickled coldly down his back, making him shiver. More drops came through. They pattered on fallen leaves. The clearing began to whisper to their sound.

In a few minutes it would be hissing and they would be soaked to the skin. They would also be alone and in darkness, for as Badger went down the steps, taking his lamp with him, the night crept back through the trees. Clouds had blotted out the moon.

If they were to be marooned in a strange part of the woods, Rupert wouldn't know where to begin looking for Katy again. He might not even find his way home. Porko was thinking the same thing about *The Dainty Duck.*

"Badger, Badger." Rupert and the pig hurried after him. "You wanted to know who we are and what we're doing here," said Rupert, stopping at the top of the steps.

Below them Badger was about to go through the doorway. He held the lamp up. "Come along then, and tell me about yourselves and, what was it? Frying parrots? Sounds rather unpleasant."

Rupert and Porko needed no second invitation. They scampered down the steps and through the door before Badger closed it against the night and the storm. The tennis racket lay forgotten where Rupert had left it among the roots.

Biffing the Enemy

The tunnel was dry, with the slight musty smell you get when a place isn't used much. Papery leaves rustled underfoot. Here and there roots hung down from the roof like coarse cobwebs. Badger led the way while Rupert recounted the night's adventures from the time Katy was taken by the Grabbly and he vowed to find and rescue her.

When he got to the point where *The Dainty Duck* anchored itself in the woods, he let Porko take over the story. By this time they had walked a long way. They rounded a corner and found themselves in a brightly lit kitchen.

"Come along in and sit down," said Badger, indicating a pair of armchairs on either side of an open fireplace. A brass toasting fork was propped up on the stone statuette of a reclining lion in front of the grate. The lion's sleeping head rested on crossed paws.

From a sideboard Badger took bread, plates, knives, a butter dish, and a jar marked Best Strawberry Jam and carried them to the fireside. He poked the gray embers of the fire into a glow. When everything was arranged to his satisfaction, Badger pulled up a third armchair from behind the table.

The kitchen was warm, with a homely clutter of furniture and odds and ends. As it filled with the smell of fresh toast, Rupert felt drowsiness creeping up on him. He closed his eyes.

A strange picture began to form in his mind that made him feel very uneasy. It was as if he was surrounded by green smoke, and from somewhere beyond it came humming and whirring sounds. The smoke cleared and he was looking across a great space at the tiny figure of Katy in a torn nightgown. She was trying to run toward him and was calling his name pitifully, "Rupert, Rupert!" But every time she ran a few steps, shadows closed around her and pushed her back. The green smoke returned, blotting out the vision. For a moment longer he heard Katy calling him, and then her voice faded away and was gone.

Rupert opened his eyes with a start. Katy was in deadly peril, and this was no time to be falling asleep. He looked round the room as if she might be there, but no. Porko was snoring softly, his mouth open.

"We must be going," said Rupert, struggling to sit up. "Come on, Porko, wake up."

The pig made a trumpeting sound, closed his mouth, and made a few chewing motions before his eyes opened.

"Now don't be in such a hurry," said Badger. "Do you know where to go or how to get there, or what to do if you arrive?"

Rupert didn't.

Badger picked up the plate and began to spread butter and jam on the toast. The jam was thick with whole strawberries.

"What you need is a plan." He pointed the knife at a portrait of a fierce badger hanging on the wall. "What Grandfather Badger would have called 'a plan of campaign to biff the enemy hard and biff him where it hurts.' Grandfather was a great general and a great campaigner. It was his plan that saved the day in

51

the Battle of Bald Hill Burrow in '84, when the Badgers defeated a band of marauding terriers."

Rupert looked at the portrait. The old soldier seemed to look back with farsighted eyes, resolute, purposeful, and courageous.

Badger went over to an oak chest, lifted the lid, and rummaged about inside it, saying, "This is the general's old campaign chest. Maybe there's something here to give me inspiration." He removed a tin helmet and an ancient gun with a funnel-shaped barrel. He put these to one side and went on, "Or something to 'knock them for six,' as Grandfather used to say. Aha, what's this?"

Badger lifted out a large book and studied the cover. On it was written, *How I Won the Battle of Bald Hill Burrow by General Badger.* Underneath in smaller letters it said, *With an explanation of strategies and tactics for Biffing the Enemy and Knocking Him for Six. Accompanied by Maps, Plans, Diagrams, and Charts.*

"This should give us a clue," said Badger, carrying the book over to the table. He opened it at the front page. Rupert and Porko looked over his shoulders as they finished their toast.

Badger read aloud, " 'In planning a campaign it is of the utmost importance that you have a thorough knowledge of the enemy, his whereabouts, his strengths and weaknesses, his likes and dislikes, his history and methods of conducting warfare. Only when you have this knowledge should you attempt to biff him with any hope of knocking him for six.' "

Badger stopped reading. Porko and Rupert looked at each other in dismay. Porko put into words what they were thinking. "We don't know anything about the Grabblies, except that they're horrible. How can we hope to succeed?"

The clock on the mantelpiece chimed. Badger looked at it. The face reminded him of someone, and an idea began to form in his mind. "Owl," he said to himself. He got up and checked the date on a calendar. "Of course. The Royal Birthday Party. That's it." He clapped his paws together with excitement, then started to go through the contents of the chest once more, throwing aside the things he didn't want.

Rupert and Porko exchanged looks. Porko shrugged and tapped his head.

At the bottom of the chest Badger found a bulky bag marked *War Department,* which he slung over his shoulder. He picked up the gun, put the helmet on his head, and handed Grandfather Badger's book to Porko.

"Is that the 'it' you were talking about?" said Porko about the bag.

"No. This is an ammunition pouch for the gun. We're going to find Owl. He's the one creature in the woods who will be able to help us. Usually he's nearly impossible to find—he shuts himself away with his books and scientific instruments. But this is the night of the Royal Birthday Party on the Field of Blue in the woods, and everyone will be there, including him. If anyone can think of a plan for rescuing Katy and finding *The Dainty Duck,* it's Owl."

"Whose party?" asked Rupert.

"The Royal Blue Lion. RBL, the King of the Woods."

Porko's snout wrinkled and twitched as if he was already smelling party cake and ice cream and jam tarts.

"Are you ready?" asked Badger.

"We're right behind you," said Porko.

54

The Royal Birthday Party

The front door of the burrow opened onto a glade of fine turf. On the far side a broad avenue of beeches went deeper into the woods. The storm had gone, blown itself out, or raced off in the tempestuous way of storms to batter another quiet corner of the countryside. The air smelt fresh and tangy.

Badger pulled the door shut with a brass knob in the shape of a terrier's head. He led them down the beech avenue and onto a narrow path while he told them that he had first met Owl when the bird was Chief of Intelligence for General Badger.

"That was ages ago and he's retired now. He spends all his time trying to discover the secret of turning stones and bits of old metal into gold." Badger laughed.

The path wound through the trees and around bushes in an aimless way. Rupert thought that whoever had made it must have been chasing butterflies or, inspired by Owl, been searching for the pot of gold at the end of the rainbow.

As they went, a change slowly took place in their surroundings.

The first rustlings sounded like leaves on the path, and the first shadowy movement between the trees might have been a restless plant —this part of the woods was full of enchanter's nightshade and the pink-tipped cottonwool wisps of rosebay willowherb.

The rustling was joined by a shuffling and a scurrying and a scampering. No leaves or plants sounded like that.

Rupert felt a warm breath on his neck. His scalp tingled. He wished that he hadn't left the tennis racket behind. He got ready to leap around.

"Rupert. Let me walk in front of you. I'm frightened." Porko spoke in a hoarse whisper and tugged at his sleeve.

"I wish you wouldn't do that, Porko. You're making me feel jumpy."

The scampering and scurrying merged together into a steady murmur that filled the air. It came from all sides, from ahead and behind. Shapes flitted through the trees like the shadows thrown on a wall by an open fire in a darkened room. Unseen wings flapped overhead. Porko clutched nervously at Rupert, who looked for Badger. He was a little way ahead, quite unconcerned.

"Badger, Badger. What's going on? What's making all that noise?" Rupert whispered, as eager now as the pig not to draw unwanted attention.

The woods squeaked and squealed. They chattered, chirruped, gurgled, giggled, whooped, whistled, buzzed, fizzed, fidgeted. They bubbled and seethed with a waterfall of sounds and movement.

"It's the party," said Badger. "Everyone's going. We must be nearly there."

He left the path and went through a dense thicket of hazel beginning to form nuts in green clusters. On the other side was a large clearing. Chinese lanterns hanging from the surrounding trees added to the moonlight that flooded it. The clearing was as big as a football field, and it was full of animals and birds.

The three of them stood for a long moment at the edge of the clearing. A tide of fur and feathers flowed, ebbed, and eddied across the moonlit glade. Badger studied the tide intently. His eyesight was poor and he frowned with concentration.

On the far side of the clearing was a tent standing on a rise of ground that made a natural grassy platform. The tent was blue. In front of it was a throne, empty.

Badger was asking if anyone had seen Owl. A pigeon thought she had, in a pine tree beyond the tent. They pushed through the throng of creatures, around the tent, and through a clump of birch saplings. Here there was another, much smaller clearing with a solitary pine tree in the middle. The birches were a screen, cutting off most of the noise and light from the party.

Badger stood in the gloom at the bottom of the pine peering up. "I can't see a thing up there. Can anyone see anything?"

His two companions were much more interested in trying to make out what was going on beyond the birches.

"Look at that," groaned Porko as they glimpsed waiters carrying trays of food. There was a roll of drums from unseen musicians. Silence fell in the clearing. The Royal Blue Lion stepped out of the tent. All the creatures in the clearing began to cheer and clap.

The king stood by the throne with his long tail looped over his right forepaw. He was a picture. From the tips of his ears to the tuft of his tail, he was blue—the light blue of a summer sky.

"Isn't he a lovely color," said Rupert admiringly.

The green pig sniffed and pulled at his waistcoat. "He's very small for a lion," was all he said. This was true. The king was barely as tall as Rupert's shoulder.

"Come on, you two," said Badger. "The party can wait until later. Look for Owl."

They turned away and walked around the tree. They heard Owl humming before they saw him. He was sitting hunched on a branch halfway up the trunk with his beak in a book.

"Owl, Owl," called Badger. The humming stopped, but there was no reply. "It's no use pretending you're not there. We can see you."

Owl sighed and put down the book. He

shifted along the branch, looked down at them with round orange eyes, and said, "Go away, whoever you are. I'm not here."

"It's me, Badger."

"Never heard of you," said Owl, picking up his book and starting to hum again.

Porko said, "Shall I throw General Badger at him? That'll knock him off his perch and give him something to remember you by."

"No, no," said Badger quickly as Porko lifted the book. "I'll explain what's happened, then he'll be sure to help us."

Badger took two steps back from the tree and raised a forepaw to command attention.

"It's those dreadful Grabblies," he began in a growly voice. "They've stolen a child, a girl called Katy, from beyond the woods. We must get her back. Grabblies are the curse of all creatures. They terrify our cubs night after night. They raise a wind that rips through the woods. Now they've turned to kidnapping. We must find their hiding place and destroy it before they do any more wickedness."

Badger had worked himself up until he was shouting. He stopped to calm down before going on to tell the story of Rupert's search for Katy, how Porko had joined him, and the mystery of where *The Dainty Duck* had gone to.

When he finished, there was silence except for the faint sounds of music and laughter coming through the trees from the Royal Blue Lion's birthday party.

"Well, is he going to help us or not?" said Porko impatiently. Badger waved a paw for him to keep quiet.

Finally Owl spoke. "You were right to come to me, Badger. It sounds bad, very, very bad." He stopped and raised a claw to scratch behind an ear. A feather came loose and floated down.

Owl went on, as if talking to himself. "It sounds, in fact, as if the Wizard has lost control. It's what I always feared."

"What's he talking about?" asked Rupert.

"We'll find out in a minute," said Badger. "Owl won't be hurried."

The bird was searching through his pockets. "I have a message here from Captain Bones. He managed to give it to a magpie who passed by him in the storm. It says where he's heading for." Rupert and Porko jumped up and down with excitement.

Owl's pockets were full of bits and pieces. He pulled a mouse out of one of them. "No, that's not it," he said, putting the mouse back. "The best thing is for us to join forces with the Captain, and then we can plan an attack on the Grabblies. I'll fly after *The Dainty Duck* when I find out where she's gone, and you can follow me on the ground. Oh, bother!" he said as an assortment of rusty nuts and bolts fell out of another pocket and a piece of paper fluttered to the ground.

They were watching Owl so closely that no one had noticed the wind returning. Rupert was the first to feel something—a shiver that prickled down his back.

He stiffened, eyes wide. It was a feeling he'd had once already tonight. Then he heard something like waves breaking on a distant shore, but rushing toward them.

"Listen," he said urgently.

Badger raised his long snout. "Is it the storm coming back or . . ."

Porko finished the sentence for him. "Or the Grabblies?"

Whichever it was, it was coming very fast this time. The trees were already starting to shake and moan. The air gusted about them noisily and the message from Captain Bones was whipped away unread.

"We must warn the animals at the party!" Rupert had to shout. There was a flash of light from the clearing as one of the Chinese lanterns was blown over and went up in flames. There were cries of alarm.

"It's too late," said Badger. "Get down!" They threw themselves on the ground.

A moment later the full fury of the wind rushed in upon them. The birch saplings bent over until they snapped, revealing a sight of dreadful confusion in the clearing. The tent was being ripped into blue rags. The bandstand had collapsed around the musicians. Tables were upturned and food lay ruined on the ground. Animals were tumbled everywhere. Some were being bowled, head over heels, along the ground. The cries of frightened or hurt creatures mixed with the howls and shrieks of the wind as it tore at all things that stood in its way.

Rupert twisted his head to look up into the treetops. Fearful shapes dashed through them, riding the wind. The shapes of anger, jealousy, and spite, poisoned words, spoiled deeds; bitterness, pain, and fear itself. Rupert recognized some old enemies as they whirled in a mad dance through the trees, screaming in the wind. Others he didn't know. They were ugly brutes, all of them.

Rupert couldn't bear to look for more than a few seconds. He buried his face in Badger's coat. Above the fury of the storm there was a crack as of doom. The pine tree came crashing down. Pine needles and cones showered around them in a thick blanket that blotted out the terrible sights and sounds.

Owl Points the Way

Badger sneezed. He sat up, scattering the green needles that covered them. He looked around carefully. The woods were still.

Badger felt under the needles for Porko and Rupert. "It's safe. They've gone."

Porko was very frightened. "How are we ever going to fight those horrible things?" he moaned. "I wish I was back on *The Dainty Duck* with Captain Bones, and miles away. Why did I ever come into the woods? Let's get away, please."

Katy, thought Rupert. Oh, Katy, where are you, what are they doing to you? He felt nearly as frightened as Porko. He was scratched and his pajamas were torn, but there was no turning back now. If the Grabblies were so horrible to look at, how much worse to be their prisoner.

He stood up and shook his fist defiantly at the treetops. "I'm coming, Katy! I'll find you, I'll find you, I will, I promise."

His brave words faded into the deep shadows. There was no answer, but far away the wind gusted with a sound like mocking laughter.

Even Badger had begun to feel defeated by the terrible power of the Grabblies. He lived by a simple code that life was fun, all creatures were decent in their own way, and if you never gave up on a problem you would never be beaten by it. It was the code that his father and grandfather had lived by, and it had served him well. For a little while he had started to doubt it, but Rupert's words put fresh heart into him.

"Don't worry, Porko," Badger said. "We'll find a way of fighting the Grabblies, and of winning."

There was a movement under the fallen tree. Badger bent down and broke off a branch that was lying across Owl's right wing, pressing him to the ground. The bird squawked with pain. Badger lifted Owl until he was propped against the tree trunk. The broken wing hung down limply.

Badger made splints out of twigs and carefully bandaged the wing with a strip torn from his handkerchief. When it was done Owl said, "You will have to go on by yourselves. I'll tell you what I know." His voice was strained.

Badger laid a paw on his back. "Easy now. Don't talk if it hurts."

After a moment Owl went on. "Just behind here is a stream. It will lead you through the woods to the River Worros. The far side is a bad and dangerous place, but you must cross to it. That land is called the Marsh. There are no trees and the east wind always blows. Travel through it as quickly as you can, and beware of the Bog Hoglins, beasts with great feet who rob strangers. You will come to the Sea of Storms and there on the shore you'll find Castle Dread."

Owl stopped talking and closed his eyes. It had been a great effort. But there was something important still to be said, and after a moment he continued. "The castle is the home of the Wizard who keeps the Grabblies. You must find a way to destroy them."

"He makes it sound easy," said Rupert. "But how do we destroy the Grabblies?"

Badger nodded thoughtfully. "Owl, Owl," he said gently, "before you sleep you must tell us more."

The bird whispered, "They are creatures of darkness. Fight them with light. Remember. Light." He lay back, exhausted.

Badger stood up, settling the blunderbuss more comfortably over his shoulder.

"Do we *have* to go?" asked Porko. He was sitting on the fallen tree, looking cold and frightened. Rupert put an arm around his plump shoulders and gave him a squeeze.

They found the stream and followed it. The woods seemed unnaturally quiet. Nothing dared to move after the Grabbly storm.

They walked and walked until they were in a part of the woods that Badger had never seen before. The trees thinned out before they reached the bank of the river. The river was very wide. The far bank was just a dark line against the sky.

They were wondering how they would cross when a rock in the middle moved. As it approached, they saw that it was a very large beetle with three pairs of oar-shaped legs. It drew in to the bank and, with a voice that came from somewhere near the water, it burbled, "I'm the water boatman. Do you want a ferry?"

They stepped onto the curved shell and sat down. The beetle pushed off and rowed across.

The land on the far side was as flat and bare as Owl had said it would be. Nothing moved except the wind and a thin mist that made the Marsh look gray.

The beetle raised its head. "There you are. Fares, please."

No one had thought of paying a fare. "How much is it?" asked Badger.

"Three coins or three pieces of metal."

Badger and Porko went through their pockets. Rupert didn't have any to go through. They didn't have a penny among them.

The beetle started to get angry. It slapped its oars on the water in a threatening way. "I must have my fares, or you can swim back. What's in that bag?"

"It's ammunition for the gun."

"That'll do for the fare. Three lead bullets. Or three brass cartridges. That'll do nicely."

Badger took the pouch off and felt inside. A look of puzzlement crossed his face. He tipped the contents out. They weren't bullets. They weren't even metal. Rupert picked one up. It was a cardboard tube the size of a candle. On the side was written, *Danger. Signal Flare.* He picked up another, made out of plastic. *Danger. Distress Flare.*

Slap, slap, slap went the beetle. "I don't want those," it shouted. "Give me metal."

Badger put his paw into the one pocket he hadn't turned out.

"All I have is this box I keep sherbet powder in. It's silver."

"I'll take it." The beetle snatched at the box. Oars aren't the best things for snatching with. The box flew open, letting out a dense cloud of fine sherbet powder. It was worse than pepper. The beetle sneezed, and it sneezed and it sneezed.

The beetle sneezed so fast and furiously, it began to move backward through the water.

"A-shoo. Aa-shoo, aaa-shoo. Aaaa-shoo." The beetle picked up speed, traveling like a gunboat and sounding like one too, until it disappeared from view upriver.

"Bless you," murmured Porko.

Rupert was stuffing the flares back into the pouch.

"Don't bother," said Badger. "They belong

on a sailing boat. They're no use to us, nor is the gun without bullets. I might as well throw them in the river." He sounded fed up.

Rupert finished repacking the pouch. "You've brought them this far, you might as well keep them." He stepped on something that chinked. The sherbet box was lying just above the waterline. He handed it to Badger. There was still a little sherbet inside. Badger was so pleased that he picked up the gun and the flares without another thought.

Bog Hoglins

The Marsh stretched away on all sides, a sour place of reeds, grass, and stunted bushes. There were no buildings and no signs. Away from the river the ground became soggier until it was quite marshy.

In places they sank up to their ankles in mud, cold black mud that sucked at their feet and paws and trotters and belched the smell of rotting cabbage when they dragged themselves free. There were pools of stagnant green water edged with rushes. Bubbles rose slowly from their depths to gather and float on the top like toadspawn or burst with the stench of dragons' breath. The east wind moaned beneath the empty sky, bringing the chill of winter.

Porko wasn't in shape for steady exercise.

He was soon lagging behind. The other two remembered Owl's warning that this was no place to waste time and wanted to push on. But eventually they had to stop to rest. They lay down close together for warmth beside one of the green pools, too tired to talk.

Bubbles were rising and bursting—*Plink, plink, plink, plop, squelch,* and then something that sounded like a straw sucking the last froth from a milkshake: *Thlooorp.* The dragon's breath was stronger.

"Pooh," said Rupert, sitting up. The thlooorping stopped.

He looked at the pool. Reeds hid most of it from view. Faint ripples disturbed the green slime on the part that could be seen. Rupert lay down, moving slightly so he could watch the pool. There was something about it that made him uneasy.

Plink, plink, thlooorp. The reeds were parted. Rupert found himself looking into a yellowish piggy face on a head like a squashed melon. It had a protruding snout like Porko's, but it was covered with warts and bristles. The eyes were red. The reeds beside it parted and another face of the same sort appeared.

"Well, what do we have here, then?" said

the first creature. The mouth when it spoke was wide enough to put a foot in.

"Dunno, Bogle," said the second creature. "What do they think they're doing sleeping on our front lawn?"

"We'll see about that, Hogle. Just let me get Wogle and we'll sort them out."

The faces disappeared behind the reeds.

Rupert was up and shaking Badger and Porko. "Wake up, wake up. Quick. It's the Bog Hoglins."

"What? Where?"

"Behind those reeds. In the pool. Come on before they come back. They're terrible. Great teeth and red eyes. Come on."

They ran.

Thlooorp-splash, thlooorp-splash, thlooorp-splash. Three Bog Hoglins came leaping over the reeds and landed on the tufty grass. They had piggy bodies and the back legs of frogs so they could jump high in the air.

One of them shouted, "Hey, you! Come back here, we want to see you."

If they had been three cats asking mice to stay to dinner, they would have had a more promising reply. Badger, Rupert, and Porko fled for their lives.

74

It was heavy going through the long grass and the mud. Badger pounded along with the tin helmet bouncing on his head and the pouch flying behind.

Rupert felt the air burning in his throat as he gasped with the effort of keeping up.

Porko, beside him, slipped in the mud and would have tumbled, but Rupert shot out an arm and steadied him. He looked back. The Bog Hoglins were gaining on them. They jumped, hit the ground, and jumped again. Their snouts were like gun barrels and their red eyes burned.

"Come on," panted Rupert. "We've got to get away." The pig grunted, too out of breath to speak. Rupert dragged him into a run. On they went. The sounds of the pursuing Bog Hoglins grew louder, and Rupert didn't dare look back anymore.

He didn't see Porko slip the next time until it was too late. "Help," squealed Porko as he fell headlong in the mud. "Help!" he shrieked as he felt scaly hands grasping him roughly by the legs.

Badger and Rupert stopped. The three Bog Hoglins had captured Porko and were dragging him away. Porko was covered in clinging mud. He opened his mouth to cry

75

"Help" a third time, but the only sound that came out was a sob.

"Come on," said Badger grimly. Rupert needed no urging. They raced back. Rupert grabbed hold of Porko and tried to pull him free while Badger set about the marsh creatures with his great claws.

Backward and forward they struggled. Once, twice Rupert was sent flying by kicks from the Bog Hoglins' long legs. Each time he got up and threw his arms around Porko. The third time he was kicked down, Badger went sprawling beside him. He had been temporarily blinded with a handful of mud and then tripped up.

The Bog Hoglins seized their chance. Holding Porko between them, they leaped high into the air and came down ten paces away. They leaped again and again.

Rupert tried to run after them, sliding and floundering in the mud. "Come back," he cried. "Oh Porko, Porko, come back."

It was no use. The marsh creatures were getting away. Badger stopped Rupert. Tears were running down Rupert's face making streaky lines in the mud. "We must rescue him.

We've got to get him back," and he clenched his fists and beat them against Badger's chest.

"Steady now," said Badger, and his voice was gruff and low. "We will get him back, but we need help."

"I'll find him. I will, I will."

Gently Badger turned Rupert around and pointed. Through his tears Rupert saw a distant castle on a rock around which the sea surged. Castle Dread.

"We can't do it by ourselves," Badger said. "If we go on we'll find Captain Bones. Then we'll come back for Porko. Please, Rupert, we must go on."

"Can't we try to get Porko first?"

"Where do we start? Where've they gone? How do we catch them? We must get help."

Rupert couldn't bear to leave Porko, but he knew that Badger was right.

As he let Badger lead him down the lonely track, two clouds appeared unseen in the sky behind them.

Castle Dread

The rock was entirely surrounded by sea. It was connected to the land by a narrow causeway with a drawbridge at the far end. A path zigzagged up the cliff face to the castle. The rock and the castle were the color of ashes. Gray. The sea was gray. It heaved restlessly, driven by the east wind.

Rupert shivered. The castle was a forbidding sight, but in a strange way it was also a welcome one because this was where his quest would end. Katy was here, he knew it. Somewhere inside those gray walls she was held prisoner. Rupert wished a thought to her. Hold on, Katy, I'm nearly there. He would go in and find her, and then he would return for Porko.

They crossed the causeway and started up

78

the path. It was steep, and it doubled back and forward across the rock face as it climbed. They reached the top and the castle stood before them, gray and massive.

Badger got down behind a boulder. It wasn't the sort of place where you march up to the front door and knock. He wanted to see if there was any other way in. The front wall of the castle rose as sheer as the rock face. There were no windows or openings of any kind apart from the door. Spaced along the top of the wall were three towers.

"There may be a way in through those towers," said Rupert.

"How do we get up there?" asked Badger. "I don't suppose there's a ladder lying about. That would be too much to hope for. Let's have a look around the side anyway to see what's there."

Before Badger could set off, Rupert clutched at his coat with a gasp and pointed at something lying on the ground beside the path. "What is it?" asked Badger, alarmed. Rupert darted forward and picked up a velvet ribbon the color of poppies. "Is that all?" said Badger, relieved it wasn't a Grabbly snake.

Rupert held the ribbon in both hands, grinning from ear to ear. "It's Katy's, that's all. It means she's here. We've come to the right place!" He laughed with excitement for the first time since they had set foot and paw on the Marsh.

"Well," said Badger, "the sooner we find her the better." And he pulled the tin helmet low over his eyes before making a dash for the right-hand corner of the castle wall. He dodged from boulder to hollow to boulder in good military fashion.

It was as well that Badger stopped to take a cautious look around the corner because if he had kept going it would have been the last anyone saw of him. The side wall of the castle was built right on the edge of the rock. There was not even a ledge where one ended and the other began. It was a sheer drop down, down, down to the sea licking hungrily below.

"Oh my giddy grandfather," gasped Badger. He pulled out the remaining piece of his handkerchief and mopped his brow. "I've no head for heights. Give me a hole in the ground any day. You know where you are with a hole."

They crossed to the other side, but it dropped away as steeply and suddenly as the first one.

"That's it, then," said Badger. "We've had it. Unless we do march up to the front door and knock. What do you think?"

"I don't think the front door is a very good idea."

"No, I suppose not. We'd probably end up in the dungeons."

"Or somewhere worse. Look up there."

There was a cloud in the sky moving rapidly over the Marsh toward the castle. They watched it get closer and larger. Earlier in the night Rupert would have waved to attract attention. He had learned since to be more cautious.

"Only one thing has a shape like that," hissed Badger.

Rupert didn't need reminding. He recognized it. In his sleep it had appeared as a flapping overcoat that flew, the way it was flying now, as if seeking something to wrap around and smother. He pressed himself against the cold stone.

The overcoat wasn't after him tonight. It headed for the central tower on the wall and disappeared through the opening.

Badger said, "We've come to the right place all right, though we're no closer to getting in."

"Yes, we are. It's given me an idea." For a moment Rupert had been nearly carried away by the old fear that Grabblies inspired in him: a desperate desire to run, a pounding heart, and a twisting in the tummy. But he had managed to come this far because he believed they could be fought and beaten, and this belief overcame his fear. He spoke with a new determination. "This wall is very rough. We can climb it and get into the castle through that tower."

Rupert went first. The stones provided plenty of hand- and footholds. The corner sloped inward as it rose, so that going up was more like climbing a steep staircase than scaling a sheer wall. When he reached the tower he pulled himself in through the window opening. Badger climbed with his eyes shut and only opened them when he was on top of the castle and felt the solid and level floor of the tower under his paws.

The tower stood on a flat roof, which they reached through an open doorway. They made for the central tower, keeping close to the low wall at the edge of the roof. In the middle of the roof, to their left, was something that looked like a very large television aerial covered in a net of shiny wire. It quivered slightly, as if ready to turn in any direction. Neither of them had ever seen anything like it, but they weren't in the mood to hang around guessing what it was.

The tower in the middle was bigger than the first one. They peered in through its doorway. There was no floor, only a great hole as dark as a well with steps leading downward. Rupert went in to explore while Badger sat on the low wall outside to get his bearings.

The Marsh stretched away, a gray desert. There was no sign of life, no sign of their journey across it, and no sign of his beloved woods. Up here the east wind was stronger. It pulled and pushed at him. Out of the corner of his eye he saw the flicker of movement.

"Rupert, Rupert," he called urgently. Rupert popped out of the darkness at the top of the stairwell. "Quick," said Badger, "help me inside. Another Grabbly is heading this way. We must find somewhere to hide."

Rupert waved his hand expressively at the bare walls of cold, rough stone inside the tower. "There's nowhere here to hide. But these steps in the floor probably go all the way down to the bottom of the castle. If this is a chimney and we're at the top, there'll be a fireplace down there we can escape from."

"If not, there'll be a door. Steps always end in doors," said Badger, brightening up at the prospect of going to ground. He made a rush for the top step. Rupert stood aside to let him go first, then followed.

In a twinkling they had vanished, and the tower was left waiting for its next visitor. Badger, well aware of what that visitor would be, went down the steps at breakneck speed, bounding from one to another. The steps went round and round in corkscrew fashion.

He stopped without warning and Rupert fell into his thick fur coat. "Steady on," said Badger, stumbling under the extra weight. "You'll have us both head over heels."

Rupert's face was buried in the deep fur between Badger's shoulder blades. It smelled of apples and peppery spice. He opened his mouth to answer, "Thorry. You thtopt thow thunnery."

"What's that?"

Rupert pushed himself back and repeated, "Sorry, you stopped so suddenly."

Badger straightened. "That's because of the light. Can you see it?"

A strange glow was rising up the stairwell from below, faint and pulsing unevenly. The steps immediately below them were picked out by dark green shadows. A little way down the dark green changed to jade, then emerald. The light moved over the stones restlessly, now pulsing brighter or darker, now flickering as if about to go out.

"It couldn't be a fire, could it?" asked Badger. He held a paw out over the drop to feel for rising heat.

"You mean this really might be a chimney?" said Rupert. "It's very big for a chimney."

"There might be a very big fire at the bottom of it," pointed out Badger.

"Then we'd better go back."

"We can't," said Badger. He threw a glance over his shoulder as if expecting to see the Grabbly. There was nothing there . . . yet. But any moment now the Grabbly was going to flap and fumble into the opening above and follow them down. They had to press on or find somewhere to hide.

Badger drew his paw back. He looked at it

and passed it under his nose to sniff. "There's no heat coming up, or smoke." He sounded puzzled.

"Maybe it's not a fire," said Rupert. "I've never seen one burn that color."

"What else could it be?" said Badger.

"I don't know. It looks like . . ." He stopped. He was going to say lightning, but you couldn't have a thunderstorm at the bottom of a chimney. ". . . electricity. I once saw flashes come out of a plug when the wires were crossed. But they were blue."

There was a faint scratching, a crackling from below, no louder than a mouse running over newspaper. Rupert leaned over to listen. Too far. He overbalanced against Badger, who was caught unprepared. They fell down the steps together in a slow somersault. As he turned over the first time and looked up, Badger was sure he saw a shapeless something creeping after them. Then they were falling fast.

The fall went on and on before they crashed into an obstacle and stopped and lay still. Rupert thought in a daze, Just another few steps and I'll be there, wherever Katy is. But he was too stunned to move.

Green for Danger

For a time that seemed an age but was only a dreadful moment, Rupert thought he was back in bed having a bad dream. He was dazed by the fall and lying awkwardly beneath a weight that pinned his legs to the ground. The clang that Badger's helmet had made when it hit the stone wall echoed and re-echoed in Rupert's ears. There seemed to be something wrong with his eyes. He saw stars swim like fishes in the sea of night. Then the stars swam away to reveal a horrible dripping blanket, worm-gray, which flapped sightlessly through the air toward him.

Rupert struggled, fighting against the unseen forces that always tried to hold him helpless in bed in the face of approaching doom. He managed to heave himself free.

He sat up and felt around in the dark for a light switch. He touched stone where there should have been a bed sheet, a furry mound where there should have been a bedside table. The furry mound groaned, "Oh, my poor head. Ooooh."

Then Rupert remembered where he was. "Badger," he called in an urgent whisper. "Badger, there's a Grabbly here. What shall we do?"

Badger groaned again. "Uumh."

Rupert grasped what he thought was a foreleg and shook it vigorously. "Badger, quickly, wake up. The Grabbly. It's about to get us."

But to his surprise the blanket flapped past them and sank out of sight.

Rupert got to his knees and crawled forward till he felt the sharp edge of stone where the floor ended. He craned his neck. Green light flickered dimly around the stairwell. It was coming from one place, an opening, not far below. The steps ended there, and the Grabbly, outlined now by a shimmer of green, flowed stickily through the opening.

Rupert relaxed and sat back on his heels.

He noticed that he and Badger had fallen into an alcove off the flight of steps. It was probably a passing place and was just deep enough to hide them.

"Who hit me, what hit me?" Badger sounded punchdrunk.

"It's all right. We're safe for the moment. How do you feel?"

"Terrible," replied Badger, putting both forepaws under the tin helmet to rub the bump. "But nothing to the way the other fellows will feel when I find them. Did you see who they were?"

"It wasn't anyone," said Rupert. "We slipped and fell down the stairs and ended up in this cubbyhole." The only answer was another groan. After a while he went on. "Do you remember me shouting to you just now?"

"The Grabbly," Badger said as the memory came back.

"It followed us down but it wasn't chasing us. It was heading for the bottom, where the light is coming from. There is a fireplace there, or a sort of doorway. It will be our way into the castle."

Badger shuffled to the edge to look. Still

rubbing his head, he grunted, "All right, but you go first this time."

The steps made two full spirals before ending just short of the opening. This was farther than it sounds because the chimney, or tower, had widened out so much. The air was chilly. Damp oozed out of cracks in the walls and trickled or dripped onto the steps. Patches of mold grew darkly, giving off a rotten smell.

Rupert picked his way carefully for fear of slipping again. At every half turn of the stairway Badger paused to peer skyward. Without thinking, he had unstrapped the blunderbuss and was holding it firmly.

Down, down they went into the well of green light. Sounds rose about them. Crackles, hisses, drippings, gurglings, tickings, burblings.

Rupert stepped off the last step onto the stone floor. Badger joined him. The opening was ahead. It was as wide as a farm gate and about as high. The top curved in a shallow arch. Badger and Rupert exchanged a glance, wordless but full of meaning.

Rupert took a deep breath, then he darted forward and through the opening. It was as if he'd passed through a curtain. Badger couldn't see what had become of him. The green light danced in the opening, revealing nothing.

Rupert found himself on a landing. It was large and quite bare, and there was no Grabbly in sight. He walked up to some heavy railings at the front of the landing, stepping softly. They were set close together and he couldn't see through them properly, at least he couldn't see anything that made sense. It was partly the light. Green flashes sparked and arched high overhead with the dazzle of lightning. There was a box by the railings and he climbed onto it slowly.

What he saw grabbed his attention so strongly that he didn't move, even when Badger ran out of the bottom of the tower.

"All clear, eh?" said Badger, looking around and lowering the gun. There was no reply. "I said, is it all clear?"

Rupert stuttered with excitement, "Jus . . . jus . . . jus . . . just look at that. Did you ever see anything like it?"

Badger was tall enough to see over the railings. The fur between his shoulder blades lifted in an angry ruff. Badger hadn't seen anything like it before, and wished he hadn't seen it now.

The landing they were standing on was at

the end of an enormous room. "Room" was the wrong word. It must have been the great hall of the castle, larger than a church, higher than a tree, wider than a barn, longer than a rope. It was huge.

So was the floor. Football, basketball, hockey, tennis, and bowls could have been played across it all at the same time without any of the balls getting into the wrong game. Perhaps golf too on the far side where the hall dimmed into the distance.

None of these things was going on.

In the middle of the floor was a huge gray metal box. Faint sounds came from it, humming and clicking. Crouched around the bottom of the box were benches of small machines, and at each one sat a small hunched figure. It was difficult to make out what was going on, but the small machines were the source of the light.

Suddenly one of the machines began to crackle and spark. Smoke puffed out of the back of it. With a loud bang, a bolt of intense green burst from the machine into the air.

The flash lit up the great hall. The figure that had been working the machine turned away from it with a toss of the head that caused Rupert to catch his breath in recognition. Rupert wanted to see more, but his eyes were drawn irresistibly up and up with the green flash as it soared toward the roof.

It lit up the wooden roofbeams. There was something odd about them. Their shape. They were bent and lumpy. Not true and straight as beams should be. Then Rupert saw with horror that the lumps were hanging from or crouching on the beams. Some of them were moving.

In another instant the harsh green light flooded the underside of the roof and the hundreds of Grabblies clustered batlike there. The light, although it burned for only a few seconds, worried them. They stirred together as if a breeze had lifted a scattering of fallen leaves.

Rupert glimpsed again the foes of many a nighttime struggle. The wreckers of the Royal Blue Lion's birthday party were there. So were many others, humpbacked goblins, furniture that moved across creaking floors, the cracks that lay doggo on ceilings until the lights were out, shark-snakes that waited in drains just beyond the bend, and the really fearful ones that lived in shadows and let you know they were there, but never let you see them until the night they did and then you were dead.

The green flash struck one of the roofbeams. It stayed there. Within it there appeared the outline of a rat with beating wings. The light was changing form. It was becoming the rat, and as it did so the green faded and went out. The lofty spaces of the hall plunged back into darkness.

Rupert clutched at the railings. His mouth was dry and something was squeezing his tummy. There was only one thing that stopped him from running—the figure that had turned away from the machine with a familiar toss of the head.

Rupert looked down from the landing and picked out the machine that had flashed. The tiny figure in front of it was sitting with bowed head hidden by a sweep of hair.

"I shouldn't have spoken so soon," snarled Badger through drawn lips. " 'All clear!' Hah. It's as clear as a nest of wasps. I never thought there were so many Grabblies in the whole world. What do we do now?"

Rupert Finds Katy

They crept down the staircase at the end of the landing to the floor below. At the bottom they crouched in the shadows. "Getting across this floor worries me," said Badger, opening his paw and fanning his claws in a gesture that took in the vast open space, the lack of cover, the huge metal box with its unknown hazards, and the menace of the Grabblies hanging above in the dark—maybe ready to fall on them at any moment.

"We could run over there in no time," said Rupert.

"And if we're spotted, we're caught in the open with nowhere to hide. No. We'll have to think of something else."

There was a fear in Rupert's mind that had

been growing since they entered the castle, and now he whispered it. "Badger, do you think the Grabblies know we're here? Can they spy us out?" He looked anxiously at the roof. The dark hid what was there, and Rupert looked away again quickly.

"I don't know. Maybe. We'd better be ready for trouble."

They looked around for anything that might be of help. Behind them was a door, probably the main door opening onto the cliff top. It was blocked with a jumble of old clothes, boots, boxes, and other rubbish, including what looked like a dog basket on wheels.

Badger went up to the basket and pulled out some pieces of wood.

"What's that?" asked Rupert.

"It's a cart for collecting firewood. This," and Badger lifted the wooden handle connected to the front wheels, "is for pulling and steering. In bad winters the wheels can be replaced with skis to go over the snow."

"Skis," said Rupert thoughtfully. He poked about in the jumble until he found a walking stick with a rubber tip. He climbed into the cart and pushed on the floor with the stick to make the cart trundle forward.

"This is how we'll cross the floor. I'll steer and you can push us along with this stick. Nothing but a galloping horse will catch us, you'll see." Rupert was excited.

As Badger hauled himself into the cart he accidentally kicked a stack of wooden boxes. The top one fell to the ground with a crash and broke apart. They froze. The noise echoed around them. It was bound to be heard. The seconds ticked away. A minute passed, and nothing happened. Slowly Badger and Rupert relaxed and settled themselves in the cart.

Off they went. There was another tense moment when they emerged from the shadowy area around the door and stairs and onto the main floor. No one challenged them, and the moment passed.

The rubber tires were half flat. They hissed over the stone floor. One of the wheels squeaked rustily as it turned. Hiss, squeak, hiss, squeak. Badger's stick struck the floor. Hiss, squeak, thump; hiss, squeak, thump, they went. They picked up speed, and in the still air of the great hall they created their own wind, which traveled with them. Rupert stood at the front, holding the steering handle and keeping a close watch for Grabblies above and to the sides.

"Look out!" cried Badger as, without warning, another green flash exploded from the machines and soared up to the roof.

Instinctively Rupert ducked. The cart swerved. He tried to correct it and they lurched over onto two wheels. The tires screeched and for a minute it was touch and go whether they were going to turn over completely.

Badger kept them upright with the stick, and he pushed them along faster and faster. Both were certain that this time they would be discovered. Anxiously Rupert scanned the hall to see from which direction they would be attacked. The log cart bounced and bucked across the floor, its hissing and squeaking and thumping noises blending into a rushing squeal like that of an angry cat.

The green light faded. They were going to get away with it again because now they had nearly reached the benches. Rupert steered for the hunched figure.

"Badger, stop pushing. We're there." The cart rolled to a halt. Rupert leaped out.

"Katy, Katy, I've found you," he shouted joyfully, not caring if any Grabblies heard him. "I'm sorry it took me so long, but I'm here now."

The girl jumped as if she had been stung. She stared at Rupert in disbelief. He gave her a hug and stood back to have a good look at her. She looked very tired and frightened. Her face was smudged where tears had run down her pale cheeks. Her nightgown was torn and her bare foot was dirty.

"I've been terribly worried about you," Rupert went on. "Everyone has. It's so good to see you. Are you all right?"

Katy's expression changed. It was like the sun rising on her face. Her eyes sparkled and her cheeks took on a pink glow. "Oh Rupert, Rupert!" she cried, flinging herself at him. He found himself being hugged and squeezed and kissed on both cheeks. Katy was laughing and crying at the same time. "Oh, Rupert," she said again, making the name sound like a bite out of a nearly ripe apple, a sharp sweetness on the tongue. "I'm so pleased you've come. I knew you would, but I was terribly afraid they would try to stop you." She shook the hair out of her eyes with a slow, sideways toss of the head that showed her tiredness.

"I found this outside the castle," said Rupert, handing her the red velvet ribbon. "And you left this behind." He put his hand inside his pajama top and brought out the slipper. Katy lifted her foot. Rupert put the slipper on it, and Katy began to laugh and cry again.

Behind them Badger cleared his throat. "Ahrrumph, rrumph." A crowd of children had left the machines they had been working and silently gathered around them. There were about a hundred altogether, boys and girls of different ages, all wearing nightclothes and all drooping with tiredness.

Rupert introduced Badger to Katy. "I would never have got here without his help," he said. Katy kissed Badger on his furry cheek.

Rupert was bursting with questions for her. "What's going on here? Who are these children?"

"They . . . we . . . are prisoners of the Wizard."

"Why? What does he want you for?"

"We were all kidnapped by Grabblies and brought here to work for him. He makes everyone work day and night, programming his giant computer. That thing there."

The gray box, even bigger close up, hummed and clicked and whirred.

"The Wizard? Yes, Owl warned us about him. He controls the Grabblies, doesn't he? But why does he have to kidnap children? Lots of my friends would give anything to work with computers. They wouldn't have to be kidnapped."

"This is different," said Katy, leading Rupert and Badger along the benches. The machines on them were terminals for the computer. They seemed ordinary enough, a keyboard and monitor combined in a gray plastic case. Underneath the monitor screen was the trademark, a pointed hat with a star and moon.

Katy said, "The Wizard is trying to make the most powerful computer in the world so that everyone will have to do what he wants. He has discovered that our dreams, the dreams of children, have magic in them and he's capturing them.

"But he doesn't want the nice dreams. It's the bad ones he's after, the nasty, frightening nightmares, because they have a horrible energy that can drive his computer and give it tremendous power.

"The Wizard has put an aerial on the roof to trap nightmares as they fly through the air, and he's kidnapping children to program the nightmares into the computer.

"It's wicked and we must stop him."

"You're right," said Rupert, "we must. But there's something I don't understand. I thought the Grabblies *were* nightmares that had escaped from the dream world and come to life."

"They are, in a way," said Katy. "The Wizard can't do all this by himself. He needs help to do the dirty work. When he traps a very strong and powerful dream, he has it changed into a Grabbly. There's a special switch inside each terminal that makes the change, and when it happens there's a green flash.

"The Grabblies do everything the Wizard wants. They can tell which children are best for this work by the way they dream. The Grabbly that brought me here was really after you, but I got in the way so it took me instead." Katy shrugged her shoulders.

Then she went on with a sudden sense of urgency, "The programming is going to be finished in a day or two, then the Wizard will start to take over the world. And do you know what he's going to do first?"

Rupert stared at her and shook his head blankly.

"He's going to take all the good dreams and lock them away because he hates them. Every night every child in the world will have a nightmare. Every night!"

Rupert was shaken with horror. He put his hand out to steady himself and touched a keyboard. It suddenly came to life, chattering like a monkey. He jumped back. Figures and letters and strange symbols streamed onto the screen. Row after row of them, a stuttering of electronic wizardry, a torrent of meaningless information. The screen filled and overfilled. Somewhere inside the machine a wire overheated and a chip failed. There was a spluttering sound and a burning smell that pinched the back of his nostrils. The screen blacked out.

"Cover your eyes, quickly," said Katy in alarm.

Without further warning a green flash exploded from the machine. The air was buffeted by the force of its rush toward the roof. When Rupert opened his eyes he saw a ragged tramp taking form within the green light.

A little boy began to whimper with fear.

"We've got to get away from here as quickly as possible," said Rupert.

"And the other children? What about them?" asked Katy.

"They must come too. No one must stay."

Escape

"We must hurry before the Wizard catches us," said Katy. "He's sure to come soon to find out why we've stopped work. Then there'll be trouble."

Rupert and Badger began to organize everyone. The smallest children were put in the log cart, and four of the biggest boys were teamed to push and pull it. The rest of the hundred children were to follow close behind in pairs. Rupert explained the route they would take—across the hall, through the front door, and down the winding path. He decided not to say anything about the trek they would have to make across the Marsh. Time enough when they got there.

"Everyone set?"

There was a chorus of "Yes" and "Let's go."

A door opened at the other end of the hall. Red light splashed onto the floor. A toad hopped through the doorway and stopped on the edge of the red pool. It was the size of a dog. A pulse throbbed in its throat below a mouth big enough to swallow a cat. The toad's eyes watched them, and grew and grew.

"Is that . . ." began Rupert.

"No," said Katy. She was staring fearfully at the doorway, fists clenched, face pale. "But that is."

The Wizard came through the door. He was tall and thin, wrapped around in a cloak of midnight sky beneath a pointed hat.

"It's too late," wailed a sad-faced girl. "We'll never get away now." Others started to cry.

Rupert felt that if he didn't act straightaway all would be lost and the Wizard would have gained another computer slave. There was a power in the hall that set the back of his neck tingling in alarm. Delay would be fatal. Already he felt a weight on his shoulders pressing him down, rooting his feet to the floor.

With an enormous effort he turned away to

face the children who were standing in a group around the cart.

"We can escape. It's not too late," he shouted. The children didn't respond. They had become sleepily quiet and their eyelids were drooping.

Desperately Rupert gave two nearby children a shove and yelled in their faces, "Wake up, wake up!" They didn't seem to hear him. "Please, don't go to sleep. We'll never get away."

Badger bounded up. "It's the toad. Don't look at its eyes." He began to push and shove the children, turning them around. "We must break the spell," he panted at Rupert. "If you can get the cart moving, it might do the trick for the rest."

Rupert hurried a listless Katy over to the cart. He put his hands on her shoulders and shook her till she blinked awake. "Katy, Katy, listen. We must get away *now*. Start pulling the cart, and Badger says whatever you do, don't look at the toad. It's hypnotizing us."

More and more of the children were coming to under Badger's rough handling. He told them to line up in pairs, each with a hand on the shoulder of the child in front, with the first two holding on to the cart. Katy grasped the handle of the cart and heaved. It was full and very heavy. Rupert put his shoulder to the corner. There was a drawn-out squeak as the wheels turned, ever so slowly.

The Wizard spoke, his words falling upon them like water dripping from an icicle. "I am Ram, Wizard of Dread. Who dares disobey me?"

"Ignore him," shouted Badger. "Run for the door under the staircase."

The big boys, now fully awake, threw their weight against the cart. It rolled forward faster, hissing and squeaking. The cart picked up speed. Pullers and pushers broke into a trot. Rupert sprinted ahead to guide them. The pace accelerated to a gallop. A string of children, linked hand to hand to the back of the cart, became a wriggling, running centipede. Badger brought up the rear to make sure no one was left behind.

The Wizard could hardly believe what was happening. He lifted his arms till they were pointing stiffly upward, then intoned in a furious voice,

"Grabblies, harken to my call,
Ensnare these children in the Hall.
Bind with nets of fear and pain,
And drag them back to me again.

"But first terrify them and scarify them and
horrify them to sorrify them, till their teeth rattle and they never think of escaping again." His
voice cracked into laughter. It was laughter
that had no joy in it, only the cackle of pleasure
taken from cruelty.

A wintry wind stirred in the roof. From
every point of that dark space came rustlings,
scratchings, slitherings, hatchings. Wings,
hoofs, claws, and cracked boots flapped,
stamped, scrabbled, and creaked. Moans and
groans were in that wind, and other sounds that
the ears of children should never hear.

Badger filled his lungs. "Run, you cubs,
run like you've never run before. Run for all
you're worth."

Badger's cry had the effect of a shove in the
back. The children ran as if the devil himself
was on their heels.

Rupert reached the lobby at the end of the
hall. He vaulted the rubbish heap and landed
beside the door. He seized the handle and

turned. The door didn't budge. He looked for a key or a bolt. There was none. He tried the handle again.

The cart bumped and squealed to a halt on the bed of old boots. Katy ran forward to help, but age and lack of use had sealed the door solid.

Rupert stepped back. "It's no use. We're never going to open it in time."

"There's no other way out," said Katy. "We *must* open it."

"There *is* a way, the steps that go up to the tower on the roof. They start inside the fireplace."

Katy shook her head. "That's how the Grabblies come and go. I was brought down there." She lifted a hand and bit a knuckle at the memory. "We might get trapped, us in the middle and Grabblies at the top and bottom."

More and more children were piling into the lobby. It was getting crowded.

"We can't stay here," said Rupert. "We'll be trapped just as easily and much quicker. We'll have to take a chance on it. But it's a steep climb. Do you think the little ones will be able to make it?"

"They will if the older ones help," Katy said, making up her mind.

A sudden shriek drew them back to more immediate dangers. One of the last children in the line, a little boy named Jimmy, had fallen. He'd hurt his ankle and couldn't get up again. Badger, bringing up the rear, had run past without noticing him.

Badger heard the watchers in the lobby shout and saw them wave to him to go back. He stopped and turned. The first of the Grabblies had come into view, dropping from their perches toward the floor. They saw Jimmy at the same moment Badger did. With a bloodcurdling yell, the leading ones, the tramp with a sack over his shoulder and an alligator, made for him.

Badger dropped to all fours to make better speed. He raced back the way he had just come. The Grabblies yelled again, but they didn't curdle Badger's blood. He was a streak of gray fur and bared teeth.

Jimmy had seen the tramp and the alligator. He could nearly feel the alligator's breath on his face. He pressed himself against the floor in the hope that they would go by. No such luck. They were coming straight for him. The tramp was stretching out a grasping hand. The alligator was smacking its great jaws together as if it could already taste a tender morsel.

Let There Be Light

Badger beat the Grabblies to their prey. He scooped Jimmy up and swerved around in one unbroken motion. The tramp snarled in disappointment. The alligator bit him on the leg, because if it couldn't bite the little boy it was going to bite the nearest thing.

The lobby was packed with children, all looking for a way out and all talking excitedly. Badger put Jimmy down by the staircase.

Rupert raised his arms to attract attention. "Listen, everybody. We can't get out this way. We'll have to go the same way we came in. The steps are steep, but it won't take long."

"Look," said Katy, pointing to the landing above them. Grabblies had landed on it, barring the way. More were in the air. The tramp and

112

the alligator were crossing the floor, though slowly. The tramp was limping and the alligator had a sack tied round its jaws.

More Grabblies settled on the landing. One of them, the newly formed rat, began to creep down the curving staircase. One of the children said, "That one terrifies me when the light is turned out at home. Shoot it, Badger, please."

Badger didn't have any bullets. He unslung the blunderbuss and was about to throw it at the rat when Rupert grabbed his arm excitedly, saying, "That's it. Light."

"What are you talking about?" said Badger.

"Don't you remember? Owl told us to fight the Grabblies with light."

"Yes, but we haven't got any."

"Oh, yes, we have. The pouch there is full of signal and distress flares. When they go off you can see the light for miles." He turned to Katy. "What happens when you turn a strong light on a Grabbly?"

"It vanishes. They can't stand light."

"Exactly."

Badger pulled out a cardboard tube and put it into the blunderbuss. It fit perfectly. He let out a whoop of a war cry.

"Wish me luck," he said, lifting the gun to his shoulder and pointing it at the rat. Rupert held his breath. Badger pulled the trigger.

There was a fizz, and a ball of brilliant light shot out of the blunderbuss. It was white and red and orange and yellow with blue streaks and golden highlights. It was radiant, beautiful, and deadly. The ball flew straight for the rat, which disappeared, pop, before it had time to realize what was happening. It vanished utterly and completely, leaving no trace behind.

The fiery ball hit the staircase and burned out. Badger reloaded and fired onto the landing. Flaming light swept the landing clear. Badger whooped again. Rupert took a handful of flares from the pouch and clapped his hands. "Everyone upstairs!"

Badger went first. He took up a position where he could look out on the great hall. In the green glow from the deserted computer terminals, shadows flitted like sharks in a dim sea. A great spider holding out a web was hovering in the air, ready to fall onto Katy as she and Rupert helped the smaller children up the staircase. Badger loaded and squeezed the trigger. He grunted with satisfaction as a streak of scorching, burning crimson carried spider and web away.

Rupert had spotted the Shadow From Behind the Bedroom Door creeping up to the bottom of the stairs. He pulled the end off one of the flares, leaned over the landing railings, and lobbed it down. The tube landed in front of the Shadow, bounced once, and flared into a white-hot globe. The Shadow didn't stand a chance.

Badger loaded and fired, loaded and fired, crisscrossing the lofty spaces of the hall with streamers of light and fire that destroyed many Grabblies and drove others back in terror. The Wizard was in a dreadful state. He was shouting at the Grabblies for being cowards and jumping up and down on his pointed hat in a rage because the children were getting away. The toad, dazzled by the strong light, couldn't make anyone feel sleepy.

Rupert had a last glimpse of the Wizard picking up his battered hat and taking a furious bite out of it. Then Rupert pushed through the crowd of children on the landing, stepped into the fireplace, and with Katy began to lead the way up the winding steps.

Around and around and up they went,

climbing the chimney tower toward the roof. When he reached the passing place into which they had tumbled on the way down, Rupert stopped. "You go on," he said to Katy. "I'll stay here and wait for Badger."

Rupert counted the children as they passed, two by two. There were still a hundred of them. Their footsteps faded away. Soon afterward the light from the firework display faded as well.

"Is that you, Badger?" Rupert shouted as something big and heavy came through the opening and started up the steps.

"Yes," puffed Badger, "and I don't think it'll be long before the Grabblies follow me. Just as soon as they realize I've run out of ammunition."

"There aren't any Grabblies left, are there, after all those flares?" asked Rupert, with a sinking feeling.

"Enough to make life difficult for us, and they will if that Wizard has his way," said Badger. "Still, that's what I call 'biffing the enemy.' I'm sure Grandfather Badger would have been proud of us."

He was about to sit down for a brief rest when an angry voice reached them. It was the

Wizard outside the opening urging the Grabblies in pursuit. They must all have been getting a bit frightened because he said threateningly, "Get up there, you good-for-nothing layabouts, or I'll shine a little light into a few dark corners myself."

There was a movement down below. Rupert knelt by the stairwell. He pulled the top off a flare and dropped it. He counted to four, then primed another and let it go, counted to four, and dropped a third one.

The first flare went off at the bottom in a sunburst, followed by shrieks and howls. By the time the glare of the third had gone out, Badger and Rupert had reached the top of the chimney.

The children had gathered at the corner of the roof by the tower. They were looking at a large cloud hurrying across the sky toward the castle. It didn't behave like an ordinary cloud. It was rising and falling and frothing at the front.

"It looks like reinforcements for the Wizard," said Badger. "We'll have to move quickly." The sounds of pursuit came up the chimney. "Rupert, have you any flares left?"

"Just one."

"Give it to me. I'll fire it when the Wizard comes out. It will give you a minute or two to lead the children down the wall."

"I'm not going without you, Badger," said Rupert. "Two of us can hold them off longer. Katy, you lead the children."

Katy shook her head. This was her fight as much as anyone's and she was going to stand shoulder to shoulder with Rupert and Badger and fight it.

But it was too late. The Wizard suddenly appeared inside the tower, his pointed hat back on his head. Out he came onto the roof, stiff with rage. The toad hopped after him.

"So you thought you'd escape me, did you?" said the Wizard. "I'll teach you to run away." He called to the Grabblies and they came pouring up out of the tower like smoke.

Badger fired the last flare. It was one of the best, liquid fire with a yellow and red core and white and blue flames dancing around it. It hissed and scorched as it flew, true to Badger's aim, toward the center of the tower.

The Wizard ducked just in time. The flare passed over his head, but it set fire to the bent tip of his hat. The brilliance of the colors dazzled the toad, which screwed its eyes shut tight.

118

Grabblies scattered in panic. The closest ones just vanished, pop, like pricked soap bubbles.

The flare hit the tower and exploded in all directions in a great shower of light. The children clapped and cheered.

It was a short-lived triumph. The flare dimmed and spluttered out as quickly as a candle in a draft. To the fire-dazzled eyes on the roof, darkness slammed down like the lid of a box.

"What do we do now?" said Rupert.

"Think," said Badger. "There must be something. I wish Owl were here."

"So," called the Wizard, "not shooting at me. I think you've got nothing left to shoot with. Am I right?" He laughed his chilling laugh.

Rupert replied to Badger, "I wish Captain Bones were here with his pirates."

Katy picked up a piece of broken tile and threw it at the Wizard. It missed. "It's no good wishing," she said bitterly, "wishes don't come true."

But she was wrong.

119

The Battle

More and more Grabblies were coming up the chimney in answer to the Wizard's summons. For every one that had been destroyed by light there seemed to be three or four more to take its place. They covered the roof and filled the air, waiting to attack. The Wizard raised his arms to give the signal.

It was then that *The Dainty Duck* sailed into view in the sky behind the Grabblies. She had been the cloud Rupert and Badger had seen earlier. As she drew close, the aerial for trapping nightmares had hidden her from view.

Rupert stared over the Wizard's shoulder at his wish come true. It was a beautiful sight. The ship was straining under full sail. Froth bubbled around her bow as she sped through the air toward Castle Dread. Her battle ensign streamed in the wind. A drum was beating to call her crew to action stations.

The Dainty Duck heeled over as she veered onto a fresh course that laid her broadside onto the roof—close enough to hit with a pebble. Rupert recognized members of the crew as they ran along the deck. He saw the guns pointing and could hear the timbers creaking and the sails cracking. There was a powerful strong dream in them.

He could hear Captain Bones barking orders by the wheel on the afterdeck. And standing beside him waving a big book—that pirate in a flowered waistcoat . . . Could it be . . . It was too much for Rupert. He jumped up and down and waved back. "Captain Bones, Porko. It's Rupert. Over here."

The Wizard sneered. He was still standing with his back to the tower so he hadn't seen the ship. "You can't catch me like that. It's one of the oldest tricks there is, trying to get me to turn around when there's no one there so you can sneak away. Now listen to this . . ."

"Fire!" roared Captain Bones in a voice that carried like a brass bell.

In the next instant flame and smoke

erupted from *The Dainty Duck* as the cannons fired together in a broadside. Shot and shell and streamers of light raked the roof of Castle Dread.

The Wizard looked as though he'd been kicked in the back by a horse. His eyes popped and his mouth fell open.

The gunners on *The Dainty Duck* reloaded and fired again. The hull of the ship disappeared behind a billowing fog of gunsmoke. For a moment she did become a cloud, a thundercloud shot through with flashes and bolts of colored lightning.

Grabblies were being shot down in tatters. The Wizard was bowled over. The roof was in havoc.

Rupert, Badger, and Katy crouched with the children from the hall as the storm of battle surged and crashed about them.

The Dainty Duck sailed out of range. For a while the guns fell silent as Captain Bones brought her about to run back down the way she had just come.

Then her cannons thundered again, spitting fire and flame. Grabblies still clinging to the aerial were swept away. The aerial itself was hit once, twice, many times. It buckled as vital parts were smashed. With a screech of twisting metal it tipped over and fell down to the sea. From the depths of the castle came a muffled bang as the giant computer blew up.

Captain Bones could be heard shouting above the uproar, "Avast, me hearties. Prepare to board." There was a grinding shock as *The Dainty Duck* made landfall on Castle Dread. Pirates, led by the Captain, swung down from the rigging on ropes. They had knives between their teeth and cutlasses stuck in their belts. In no time they had rounded up the Wizard and the remaining Grabblies.

Porko was the last ashore. He and Rupert threw their arms around each other and hugged and danced in a circle.

"I didn't believe my eyes when I saw you on the ship," said Rupert. "How did you manage it?"

The pig chuckled. "The Bog Hoglins had taken me as far as their pond and were arguing over what to do with me when *The Dainty Duck* swooped down and saved me. It can't have been more than five minutes, and you had just gone out of sight."

Captain Bones said, "We were chasing one of them there Grabblies over the Marsh when the lookout spied Porko here. He makes a good landmark. Those Bog Hoglins and their friends put up quite a fight, otherwise we'd have been here sooner."

"Two rescues in one night, that's pretty good going," said Badger.

The Captain looked pleased.

They couldn't decide what to do with the Wizard and the other prisoners, although lots of bloodcurdling suggestions were made.

Badger said, "We aren't the only ones who deserve a say in what happens. Creatures all over this land have been terrorized. Only tonight the Grabblies went into Willowherb Woods where the Royal Blue Lion was having a birthday party and ruined it. I think that we should take our prisoners to the woods and have a grand meeting where everyone can decide what to do with them."

It was agreed.

"We'll sail there," said Captain Bones. "All aboard *The Dainty Duck*. Take the prisoners down to the hold and clap them in irons."

Rupert watched Castle Dread drop behind, empty now and lifeless. It seemed to have shrunk and lost its menace. Just an old barn with holes in the roof.

The Marsh slipped under their keel. Ahead Rupert could see the silvery gleam of the river and beyond it the dark line that was the beginning of the woods. The deck felt warm under his feet. The sights and sounds and smells of the ship were homely. It was good to be back on board.

A Golden Morning

T*he Dainty Duck* crossed the Marsh and the river. Once more the moon in its brilliance sparkled in the treetops of the woods passing beneath them. Close-hauled, they rounded a great oak, and there in front of them was the Field of Blue.

The Dainty Duck settled as gently as a feather onto the ground at the edge of the Field of Blue. The field quickly filled with animals and birds.

The Royal Blue Lion sat on his throne and called for silence. "We have all suffered from the Wizard and his Grabblies and we've come together now to sit in judgment on them. Bring forward the prisoners."

The nearest pair of flying pirates prodded

126

the tramp and the alligator forward with their cutlasses. They stumbled into the clear space below the grass bank, looking very unhappy.

Animals craned their necks for a better look and hissed and growled and tut-tutted when they got one. Birds crowding the trees ruffled their wings angrily.

"What do you have to say for yourselves?" said the King sternly.

"Well, Your Majesty," began the tramp, "I never wanted to be a Grabbly." He was interrupted by the howls of anger that the word produced. The tramp nervously shuffled his hat from hand to hand. The cowardly alligator cowered by the tramp's leg—the one it had bitten.

"I started life as a sweet dream. I was a schoolmaster who took a class on a nature ramble through meadows of buttercups and primroses. The sun shone. The air was full of the scent of flowers and the murmur of bees. I pointed out the beauties of nature to the children and read them little bits of poetry. It was a lovely dream." The tramp wiped away a tear at the memory. "Then something happened. I don't know what it was. The sun went behind a black cloud and a wild wind blew. The children ran away from me, and I felt trapped in a net. I heard the Wizard say, 'This is a good one,' then there was a green flash and I was changed. I hated it.''

Those animals who had hissed the tramp a minute ago were now muttering sympathetically, "Poor man," and "How awful," and "It's not his fault." The alligator was crying huge tears that splashed on the ground.

"I see," said the King. "A difficult case, that. I think we'll suspend judgment until we've heard a few more. Next."

The alligator's story, when it managed to stop crying long enough to tell it, was even sadder. Long ago it had been in a picture book, having adventures learning to swim. A small boy looking at the pictures at bedtime had enjoyed the story so much he didn't want it to end. The alligator let itself be borrowed as a dream so the story could go on while the boy slept. It was a kind alligator in those days. A change came about in the dream, just as with the tramp. The alligator turned nasty. It growled and showed its teeth and lashed its tail and chased the small boy all the way to the castle.

They were all like that. Every Grabbly that

told its story had started out as a nice, ordinary dream until the Wizard got hold of it.

"Enough," said the King. "Bring on the Wizard."

Four of the biggest pirates marched him through the crowd and up to the throne. There was a great buzz of excitement as the creatures farthest away jostled one another to get a better view, while the ones at the front shrank back. Some of the more nervous hid their heads, and one or two cubs and chicks burst into tears at the sight of him.

"Halt!" said the pirates as they reached the King.

The Wizard stood there looking much smaller than he had at the castle. Rupert decided that this was because the Wizard had lost his power. His face had the unhealthy pastiness of people who don't get enough fresh air.

The Royal Blue Lion put on his most severe expression, and said, "You are charged with the terrible crimes of stealing children, hijacking dreams, making nightmares, and spreading fear throughout the land. What do you have to say for yourself?"

The Wizard blinked. "Would you like to

buy a secondhand computer system? Very good, very cheap."

"Certainly not," said the King, offended.

"Ah, you've probably heard that I had a few teething problems with the Mark One. But I've already got plans for the next model. Forget about dream power. Unreliable and messy. All those nightmares cluttering up the place. The new one will work on something quite different. Magnetic currents."

"Enough," roared the King. "We've heard enough." He addressed the gathering. "What do you say? Is the Wizard innocent or guilty?"

"Guilty!" everyone cried.

The King sat down. He summoned his advisers to ask their opinion on the most suitable punishment. He asked Badger, Rupert, Porko, Katy, and lots of others. Eventually they reached a decision.

The King passed sentence. "It is the judgment of all the creatures of the woods that you be imprisoned in a thunderstorm for ninety-nine years, or until you mend your ways."

Captain Bones said, "I know a really nasty thunderstorm, a tropical storm, over Biscay way. It's known as Raging Jack Flash. I'll drop him off later." The Wizard was led off to *The Dainty Duck* in chains.

The Grabblies were pardoned on condition they returned to being happy dreams. And the Royal Birthday Party started up again.

The trumpeters blew a fanfare and out from behind the royal tent came a line of cooks carrying cakes, tarts, jellies, ice cream, and a covered dish that gave off a rich, steamy smell.

The Royal Blue Lion invited Rupert, Katy, Badger, Porko, and Captain Bones to join him at the table of honor. It was the best party any of them had ever been to.

Rupert and Katy ate honey cake while taking turns telling the King everything that had happened. The covered dish was placed in front of Porko and the lid removed to reveal—yes, a mound of delicious macaroni and cheese. Badger handed out little pinches of sherbet powder to an eager circle of cubs, and Captain Bones told tall tales of the seven winds.

The party might still be going on now if the night hadn't faded in the eastern sky. Captain Bones finished a story, stretched, and, with a weather eye on the morning light spreading through the treetops, said, "Well, shipmates. I can sense a dream blowing that's set fair for us. We have all the children to take to their homes before we hand over the Wizard. It's time to weigh anchor."

Everyone went aboard the ship after saying their goodbyes to the Royal Blue Lion. Porko said he had to sing a little song because his tummy felt so happy. It went like this:

"We are Pirates bold
Who are as good as gold
As we fly through the sky
In our ship of old."

"Could I try a little song?" asked Rupert with a mischievous smile.

He sang,

"Who's a jolly bigwig
With a skin like a fig
Sniffing cheese on the breeze?
Yes, it's Porko the Pig."

While everyone laughed and clapped and shouted for more, Rupert squeezed Porko until the pig gave a cheesy squeak. "Keep away from

'Thing' traps, won't you?" said Rupert. Porko giggled.

The Dainty Duck sailed to the edge of the woods, where she stopped to put down Rupert, Katy, and Badger. Captain Bones was just saying that any time they wanted to join his crew and go pirating they only had to dream the right dream when there was a squawk from inside the woods and a cry of "Wait, wait."

Owl came hopping through the trees, helped by a nephew, with something held under his good wing. It was Rupert's missing tennis racket, which had in a way started the whole adventure. The racket was different. It glowed warmly golden in the morning light.

"Here," said Owl breathlessly, passing it to Rupert. "I tripped over this just now, and I was so cross I said something in a rush without thinking and it must have been the magic spell for turning things into gold."

"It's the first time he's ever done it," said his nephew.

Owl gave a great sigh. "The trouble is, I can't for the life of me remember what I said."

A new dream filled *The Dainty Duck*'s sails, lifting her off the ground. She soared like a bird

133

toward the welcoming sky with the crew lining the side to wave. On her bow she had a new figurehead—the Wizard tied on tightly.

"It's time you were going, too," said Badger to the children. They each gave him a big hug.

Katy took the golden racket from Rupert. "Wasn't it my turn next?"

"No, it was mine," said Rupert.

"I'll race you for it." And they ran laughing through the cornfield to the cottage waiting for them in the morning time.